THE EXODUSTERS

The Man From Texas

By

Nick Jones

This book is a work of fiction. Places, events, and situations in this story are purely fictional. Any resemblance to actual persons, living or dead, is coincidental.

ISBN: 1-4033-8938-1 (e-book)
ISBN: 1-4033-8939-X (Paperback)

This book is printed on acid free paper.

1stBooks - rev. 01/22/03

THANK YOU

To God, from whom all blessings flow.

To my mother (Dessie L. Jones) and my father (Thomas J. Jones), whose union produced me.

To my Grandparents, (Will & Mary Parks), who raised me.

To my wife (Tanya R. Jones), who helped encourage me.

To my mentors, (The late Dr. Walt P. Risler and Dr. Nudie E. Williams, University of Arkansas-Fayetteville), who helped nuture my academic and professional growth.

To Amanda Nelson for typing my manuscript.

To all the black cowboys I grew up with in South Bend, Indiana, from Pre-K through the time when girls became more important than 'stick-horses' and cap guns!

TO THE READER;

This is my second short novel but, the first to be published.

I specialize in western projects about Black American men who helped develop America's Western Frontier!

Why is that important? Image. Image. The development of America's Western Frontier was the greatest growth the modern world has witnessed.

It paved the way for the Industrial Revolution and culminated in our nation's status as the world's super power!

However, the countless contributions of Black American men to this historic development have been… deliberately… omitted!

Thereby, creating an image of Black American men which is neither positive nor correct!

An image that is emblazoned in our national psyche.

Admittedly, as a scholar of America's Western Frontier, my short novels blend historical western fact with fiction. And, are written from a Black American male perspective.

However, what distinguishes my western short novels from any (similar) western short novel ever written is in every Nick Jones project, all heroes and villains are heroes and villains because of the content of their character and not because of the color of their skin.

I will always strive to give you my… ***BEST***!

Enjoy,
Nick

THE ORIGINAL… "DREAM"

Lincoln, "The Child of Labor", said, "Advancement, improvement in condition, is the order of things in a society of 'equals'. A society in which there can be <u>no</u> class who are always to <u>remain</u> laborers."

The west was nothing less than the republican solution to the problem of… Poverty. Lincoln favored homestead legislation with tracts small enough (160 acres) and cheap enough to be within the <u>common peoples</u>' grasp and, thus, aid them in achieving economic independence.

Economic independence was tied directly to land ownership and, only one part of the nation had enough surplus… land… to keep the… "Dream"… of independence alive. The West.

But, the… "Dream"… was that of a… "white"… west.

Even so, free Blacks and ex-slaves, of strong character and determination, believed in the… "Dream".

These… "unwelcomed" <u>Americans…</u> also ventured… West!

THE MYTH

In the 19th century, "newspaper reporters" and "sketch artists" sent words about and, visual images of, the "newest" pioneers in the American West.

These "reporters" used fact and fiction to "create" a "population" of White elected officials; of White law enforcement; of White developers and, of White entrepreneurs.

Thus, their primarily White eastern readers were able to identify with an "acceptable" image. Giving birth to the "white" myth of the American West.

As the "mass media" progressed, magazines, comic books, radio programs, Hollywood and television "westerns" would reflect this inaccurate and erroneous "image".

Establishing a universal myth of the American West that has existed, in one form or another, for the past 150 years!

Walter Jackson: The "first" Black cowboy in Great Falls, Montana. Jackson is reported to be the first Black baby born in Great Falls on October 2, 1887. He was never an "outlaw" or a gunfighter. Walter Jackson was reported to have been a law-abiding "top hand.".. After a successful career as a cowboy, Jackson is said to have worked for… and retired from… the railroad. The following movie (book) is based entirely upon fictional accounts.

All other characters and events are fictitious. Any resemblance to circumstances, persons living or dead, is purely coincidental.

INTRODUCTION

A harsh truth, which has been attributed to the outlaw, Frank James, could be the Epitaph Of All Western Outlaws: "I have literally lived in the saddle. I have never known a day of peace. It was one long, anxious, inexorable eternal vigil. When I slept, it was literally in the midst of an arsenal. If I heard dogs bark more fiercely than usual or, the feet of horses in greater volume of sound than usual, I stood to arms… Have you any idea of what A man must endure who lives such a life? No… you cannot. No one can… unless… he lives it for himself…"

Frank James

Outlaw

OPENING

Kissing her… he turned and walked toward the door. She had said, just moments ago, she… loved… him. That she would always love him, although he did not love her, and… had told her so… just moments… ago.

The preacher's daughter, he thought, could be quite naïve despite her maturity.

Hell, she had to realize people in his line of work did not live to a ripe old age… didn't she? He was headed for a "business" appointment… near Coal Creek… with a gentleman of the same "persuasion"… only one would leave… Coal Creek… alive!

He had been, and was, fascinated with how alive he felt, how sharp his senses "appeared" to become prior to facing… death… death today sat at a campfire drinking coffee and wearing a cherubic smile…

"Good morning, Mr. Jackson… "join me for coffee?"

"I would be pleased to Mr. Fleming, got a cup in my saddlebags." Dismounting, Walter removed the cup, walked to the coffee pot… and poured. Separated by the campfire, Jackson sat and drank deeply of the strong brew.

Time appeared to stand still for the next several minutes. Perhaps, allowing each of the "professional" killers to reflect upon how each had arrived at this point… in Hell. A hell each… had willingly chosen…

Uncharacteristically, Walter spoke first. "Duhoon willing to find another pasture?"

"No sir, Mr Jackson, he is not," answered Raul Fleming. The Jackson Duhgon gangs were competing for the riches of a territory protected by a sparse group of U.S. Calvarymen. One gang could grow "fat"… two gangs… was "one" gang too many. To avoid war between the two groups, each agreed to send their very… "best"… to resolve the issue. To the victor… for the loser… saddle and ride. Who said there was no honor among thieves?

Lowering his cup and raising his eyes, Jackson said, "I guess we best get at it."

Both men rose slowly, prepared to collect a king's ransom… or enter "Hell" with… a blazing gun.

Unloosening his holster thong, a unsmiling Walter spoke first, "They say you're good." A smiling Fleming replied, "They say the same about you. A Smirking, Jackson replied, "They're wrong." A puzzled Fleming replied, "Wrong?"

A smiling "Durango" said, "I'm the Best!"

An unsmiling Fleming answered, "Prove it, damn you"

Fleming was "good." He drew and got off a round. His slug hit the earth in front of Jackson… Jackson was the… best! He drew and got off two rounds. The first hit Fleming in the throat… slamming the dying gunfighter into the tree directly behind him. Durango's second slug tore the top off what was… once… the handsome gunman's… face.

Fleming's stench 'fouled' the air… immediately. If not sooner. Death… made him unaware that he was 'covered' in urine and… human waste.

The flies, and their nearest relatives, hurriedly, gathered for the… "nasty"… feast.

To the victor…

CHAPTER ONE

He sat staring at the half-empty/half-full bottle of "Redeye." the "old man" worked quietly behind him… rustling the eggs, beans, bacon and biscuits.

He and the boys had downed most of the coffee the "old man" had made.

The "old man," whose given name was Matthew, had risen before sunrise.

Matthew didn't mind the "boys" calling him "old man." He had lived longer… than most of them… ever… would.

Matthew like the way 'Durango' handled the gang. Just as he had in the "old days." One man in charge… a man who was strong… tough… and smart.

Matthew had met 'Durango' in Mexico, more than a year ago. 'Durango' had shown the "old man"… respect. Treated him decent… listened to him talk.

For the "foolish," Matthew Tagon was just an "old man." 'Durango' knew of his "exploits" as the leader of the Tagon gang, during the bloody (Texas) Cass County war in the '40's. Tagon had done… more… than his share o'killin!

Matthew admired 'Durango' for showing him respect… offering him a job… and 'Durango's' appreciation of his vast "business" experience.

Turning from the cook stove, Matthew said, "Grubs… ready."

"Durango," pouring himself another drink, said… nothing.

The cabin door creaked open, and Ham Doolittle stepped in. Ham had met up with 'Durango' out Arizona way. They had rode the same trail since finding themselves a hop-skip 'n a jump ahead of the Arizona Rangers.

There was a "major" misunderstanding regarding a large bank withdrawal the two, along with Sever Bound, had made from the Ancox Bank in Impact, Arizona near the New Mexico Border. The "misunderstanding" was based on the withdrawal being made 'round midnight... With guns and explosives. There were no witnesses. Regardless, Wanted Dodgers were soon... posted... for the... Jackson gang.

Ham did not know much 'bout Sever... 'cept he 'n "Durango' had been riding side-by-side since the close of the war of "Brother again Brother."

Bound nor Jackson spoke on it... much. But, since they had met, the men had made it their life's work watching each other's... back!

As 'Durango's' gaze went from the bottle ta Doolittle's face, Ham said, "Hosses ready. New man aint back yet." 'Durango' saying nothing, motioned for Ham ta take a seat. The "old man" brought over a coupla plates o'hot grub. Leaving by the back door... Matthew took a third plate out ta... Sever Bound, who was standing lookout.

Jackson and Doolittle ate heartily, and in... silence. Each had come ta appreciate "hot grub." Sometimes a "rare" commodity in their "business."

Maturity... and the nature of their... "business"... had taught 'Durango' to speak only when it was necessary. He spoke… now! “We follow the plan, won’t be no trouble. “Hole thing outa not be takin no more ‘n a few hours.” Ham responded, between copious bites o’ grub, “Shore thing… Boss. We aint had a job to wrong yet!”

“Durango,” looking pensively, said, “Always a first time… for… everything.” Ham, still eating, just nodded.

Unlike many, at that time, most of the Jackson Gang could read. They spoke, usually, as learned men… especially when required. But,… more than that, they were tough, trail smart and would… “kill”… when they had to…

Before their “business” appointment was concluded, they would have too… more than… once!

Nick Jones

CHAPTER TWO

Sever Bound, one of the… few… men 'Durango' trusted, the other being the "old man" was finishing the last of his coffee when he heard the approaching horse.

It was probably the new man Novell Jecter. Bound had his Winchester Repeater lined for who or what was coming. If'n it were not the ignorant Jecter… it… what ever it might be… was… dead!

He didn't like Jecter, but he knew why 'Durango' had brung him in… Jecter held the key to a small fortune. The "fool" knew it and played it for all it were worth. Jecter shoulda knowed something of utmost importance… 'Durango' was not a man who tolerated a fool… Sever Bound was… another.

Jecter rode up close to Sever and stopped. He remained in the saddle, astride a mount that looked and smelled better than he did, "Been outcha long?" Bound responded coolly, "Long enough… did ya get… it?". Jecter smiled, showing uneven and discolored teeth, "Get what… whatcha bees-a-talkin 'bout… Bound?". Pointedly, Sever replied, "Mr. Bound to the likes of you." Jecter, cutting his smile short, said, "Don't cha goes ta high 'n amitin me Mista Ole Novell Jecter aint a playin number two ta naw nigger… how 'bout dat!"

With eyes blazing, Sever answered, "You ride inta camp without what 'Durango' wants… that "nigga's" gonna blow a thousand holes in ya stinkin ass."

A recalcitrant Jecter responded, "Naw needs fer ya ta bee a talkin ta me dat aways. We both bees White mens."

Slowly raising his Winchester, Bound retorted, "Aint my fault… now… get!"

As he watched Jecter ride toward the Gang's cabin, he "knew" once the "business" was completed, 'Durango' would figure a way… a… how… and a… why… to kill… Jecter. Sever's only hope was that 'Durango' would assign him the task!

The Exodusters
The Man From Texas

CHAPTER THREE

He was deep in thought, which seemed to occur more often now days, as he stood outside the cabin watching the stinkin ass "redneck" approach.

He did not quibble with, nor have qualms about, any man not caring to be in his company because that man did not take to his "kind"... he wanted to and, would kill the "foul" smelling Jecter... but not without... reason... but Jecter would be just as dead!

Walter Jackson... had killed men before, in defense of his life. He was a professional gunman who lived by a strict personal code: Cross him and he would kill you! He had heard some "gunnies" say professional killin was not personal... hell... dyin was as personal as it got... wasn't it?

The outlaw side of him had robbed and stole. The outlaw side of him had not lied or cheated. Nor had he killed anyone during the commission of one of his "many business transactions." The bounty on him was $8,000 or, was it $10,000? The more "successful" he became... the harder... it became to sleep with both eyes... closed...

He needed a... reason... to kill Jecter. 'Durango' knew the ignorant fool would... eventually.. provide him with... one!

As Novell neared the cabin, he wondered how a "niggar" could have become so good with a gun... it just didn't seem "right." It went against the natural order of things. Everybody knowed that the "Good Book" said in Genesis 9:18:27 (Novell couldn't read, but someone had told him about it), that “niggars” was a-cursed and were ta be “slaves” of white folks! (The author invites the reader to read Genesis, Chapter 9 in its entirety).

One of the “justifications” for slavery in Pre-Civil War America and, a “justification” for continued racism in modern America, was/is… “it was God’s will that all Blacks be the perpetual servants of, submissive to etc., whites, because of the curse of Ham.”

(God meant no such thing.)

As painful as it may have been, Novell continued to “think.” He was saying to himself, “so ifn the “Good Book” bees true, why was “dis” niggar the head o’dis har gang? And bees so good wifa gun? Damn!”

Oh… how he wanted ta kill dis “uppity niggar,” he had already made plans to do just… that! He must be very careful… he “must” clear his mind of this thought. If Mr. Jackson, he hated having to address a “niggar” as Mister, suspected the least little thing about this planned treachery… he were dead… dead… dead!

Jecter thought he had heared some whars that “niggars” can read whitemen’s minds.

He knew that “niggars” reading a white man’s mind were also in the “Good Book”… he just couldn’t ‘member chapter ‘n verse… Novell reigned up short… square in front of… ‘Durango’!

Nick Jones

CHAPTER FOUR

A smiling Jecter, as with most "successful" sycophants, continued his discolored tooth smile as he said, "I gots what ya sents me fer… Mr. Jackson."

"Alright", was Jackson's reply. "Hot grub inside… wash… then have Mr. Tagon fix you a plate. You can eat out… here… in the fresh air."

"Yessir, Mr. Jackson… yessir."

Novell could hardly wait until he and Harley got the drops on this "uppity," proper-talkin, niggar. Together… they would kill this black bastard… fer shore 'n fer true!

Still smiling, not knowing that from the beginning 'Durango' had labeled him a traitor, Novell handed the gang's leader the much anticipated schedule of the Cavalry's Fort Walker… payroll shipment. No one would <u>ever</u> mistake Novell Jecter for a "genius"… except Novell Jecter! Unfortunately, Novell's perception of his mental abilities… did <u>not</u>… coincide with… reality! If they had… he might have surmised that he was about to eat… one of his last… meals.

Harley Gibbs, trooper, U.S. Calvary 3rd Regiment, was commanded by a Colonel Daily Ransom Walker, whose great-great-grandfather had founded the Walker settlement.

Trooper Harley Gibbs, of Fort Walker, has been 'busted' more times that the number of pimples on the ass of the fat whore he visited in Coopersville. And Big Mable, as he lovingly called her, had… a lot of… ass!

It was no secret how Harley had gotten into the military… during the Civil War, Harley had been… conscripted… After the war, the Cavalry desperately needed volunteers to patrol the violent western frontier.

The secret was… how… in "in the hell" did Harley remain in the military? Whoever knew, wasn't talking!

Had the Army been this hard pressed for men?

Regardless, here he was Harley Gibbs, the U.S. Cavalry's finest. At least in Harley's… mind! Harley… faced with 'doin moe niggar'… work. Latrine duty. Again!

The more he dug… the more… he had to dig. Awaitin… were the stables… again! Why! Just because he was a few days(?) later in reporting back from Coopersville.

Hell, were not a war goin. Were not naw "red" Injuns ta fight. Jes more marchin, drillin, patrol 'n a-cleanin.

Once he and Novell got that… payroll… 'n the reward fer dat 'niggar'… thangs was gonna be a 'hole lots different', a 'hole lots different'!

Harley Gibbs, the U.S. calvary's finest, resumed his digging… again!

Pete Cage was nearing sixty. Pete was one of Coopersville's leading citizens. The business community's… stalwart.

He rose each morning, as he had for the past twenty years, at sun-up. Put on his "store" bought teeth, shaved, took a "spit" bath and… fixed breakfast. Salt pork and beans. On Sundays and at Christmas…

he had eggs and fresh bread smothered with pear preserves. It was one of his few liberties. The other was… Big Mable!

For Pete, his work was just beyond the tattered blanket, which separated his meager living quarters from the front of the store. Cage's Feed 'N Seed were the only general store for better than a 'hundrt miles. Serving as stage depot, post office and town bank. Hell, on Saturday nights or fer big doins – Cage's Feed 'N Seed were Coopersville's answer to Tiffany's back East. Pete Cage had been honest… most… of his life. He might have stayed that way if the town's whore, Big Mable, hadn't got her hooks… inta him!

Big Mable, she were whore fer the town, the troopers at Fort Walker, and… anyone else… who had a dollar…

But… but… she were a "good whore"!

O'l Pete… he was a "smittin"… just thankin 'bout Mable gave him 'chills 'n fever'. The woman could suck the roof off a million dollar outhouse, shingles included!

Big Mable 'sucked' Pete Cage hard and often… hard and often enough to 'make' him agree to help steal the Fort Walker payroll… But not hard and often enough to make him do… murder… He hoped!

Watching the five man patrol ride out. Col. Daily Ransom Walker, the decorated (Civil War) Colonel Daily Ransom Walker, lit a cigar… and… reflected on his… 'career'.

He was pleased to be the commander of his great-great-grandfather's settlement. The settlement which eventually became… Fort Samuel T. Walker.

This was a step-up… wasn't it?

Col. Walker was not pleased to be "stuck" on the Texas/Oklahoma border… in the middle of nowhere… charged with protecting the territory with a mere handful of troops. Damn… it! If he was successful… a transfer back east… a possible promotion(?)… A "Posh" Washington assignment(?)…

The Colonel's biggest problem, besides his wife's constant "bitchin," was the roving bands of outlaws criss-crossing the border states. The Indians, by and large, were fairly peaceable. He hoped the reports he had received on the "notorious" Jackson Gang weren't… true…

And then… there was the Colonel's better half… Molly Walker. You couldn't call Molly Walker ugly. She was, after all, the colonel's wife. However, on a "beauty" scale of one-ten… she wouldn't make it…

Molly Fair, her maiden name, was educated, cultured, virtuous, and… rich… when she first met, the then Second Lieutenant, Daily Walker that cool October evening in Washington… at the Officers Ball.

She had "always" loved Washington. The culture, the sophistication, the… power…

The 'handsome' Daily would rise fast… wouldn't… he? Now, thirty-five years later, as she sat staring at the vast emptiness outside her starke bedroom's window, which was no match for the emptiness in her… heart… she was only educated and cultured… Daily had squandered… everything… else!

The Walker's marriage had been one of 'convience' the Walker name… the Fair fortune. Today, all they had was… the Walker name!

How... could... Daily Ransom Walker badly invest all that money. All her family's money... generating nothing but... heartache... in return.

On the heels of the ill-advised business ventures, came the... drinking. Life was further complicated by the long nights at Fort Walker. The lack of passion... in the starke Walker... bedroom and... no children.

Molly did not know... if... she hated Col. Walker most because of the bad investments, the slow rise in command, the drinking, the banishment to Fort Walker, or... no children. In either case, she did... hate... him!

Nick Jones

CHAPTER FIVE

It was hot… hotter than it had been for some… time. The gang rode in silence… toward Coopersville. Jecter had ridden inta the one-dog town, late the night before. The Army, using an evasive maneuver, adjusted the time of the payroll's delivery to Fort Walker, the method remained the same… by freight wagon… "Motherhened" by four troopers, a driver 'n a shot-gun guard. Ya caint blame the Army fer the lack o'vision. Never had anyone "attempted" to attack a government pay wagon 'afore. At least never along the Texas/Oklahoma border… until this day!

Jecter sat outside Cage's Feed 'N Seed drinking beer. He was on the watch… the heat was overpowering… the heat could not rival Novell's… smell. Jecter was watching foe any "unusual" movements within the small community.

An elderly veteran of the Mexican-War served as town constable. His name were Cause Walters, he earned the kingly sum of… five dollars a month. And free beer. If Cause wanted "hard" liquor, he did on occasion, he had ta pay fer… that!

Novell Jecter "thought" it must be a hell-of-a… thang ta die few five dollars. Jecter fingered the black-powder colt resting inside his waistband, and drank deeply of the golden liquid. Novell was gonna kill the o'l bastard… fer workin so… cheap.

The Jackson Gang in particular, and Walter Jackson specifically, had survived by doing the "unexpected"… when least "expected"!

Jackson reigned up, "We aint going to Coopersville. We're heading for Feathers Woods. We'll hit 'um before they get to town." Sever Bound had rid with Walter long enough to "expect" the "unexpected" But… this caught the wiley outlaw by… surprise. He had learned long ago not to question… "Durango." He didn't now…

Sergeant Bill Nary, a twenty-five year veteran, was one week short of retirement… and his pension. Presently, the 'Sarge' was fighting a war on three fronts: the heat, the flies, the "hangover." He just wanted to get this damn payroll ta the Fort… The patrol would have to, as usual, stop in Coopersville ta fill the Quartermater's order "n den on ta Fot (Fort) Walker. One moe week o'misfits, a 'drunken' Colonel, outlaw patrols… boredom. Perhaps it was his pendin Tirement, maybe it was the after affects of the cheap whiskey, whatever it was… it caused a usually observant Bill Nary to overlook several "key" factors prior to leaving the Fort… that signified… doom!

Factor One: Harley Gibbs was the first man to volunteer for the payroll detail. Harley Gibbs had never volunteered for anything in his "illustrious" military career!

Factor Two: Through a crack in the door to their living quarters, Nary had seed Colonel Walker striking… Mrs. Walker. The entire Fort knew they argued, bitterly at times, but… hitting her? The Colonel musta gotten drunker den… usual…, cause when the patrol rolled-out… maybe the Colonel would be up 'n 'bout fore noon… maybe.

Factor Three: Approaching the Beck Stream crossin, the patrol found a "dead" man blockin their path.

Close ta, mayhaps, fifty yard from the 'dead' man, Sgt. Nary signaled the payroll detail ta halt… Nary rode point, civilians Haskall (driver), and Evans (guard) were on the wagon, troopers Gibbs; Pike; and Easter brought up the rear.

Fate willed Sgt. Nary ta yell, "Gibbs front 'n cenner."

"Yessah, Sgt. Nary."

"Gibbs go 'n check da fella ta see ifn he be a gonna"! Harley dismount and sauntered toward the prostrate body… turning the "dead" man over, a startled Gibbs turned whiter… than… white.

'Durango' put the barrel of his .44-.40 in the stomach of the startled trooper, saying, "Afternoon… Harley… move 'n I'll blow a hole in ya big enough ta drive that wagon through… A near 'nauseous' Nary yelled, "What ta hell be da 'hole-up?… He dead or naw?

To the trooper's right Sever Bound shouted, "No… he aint be dead Sergeant… but you damn sure will if the boys don't drop them weapons." 'N… ah… Mr. Sergeant… shu," said Ham from behind the detail. "Ifn he don't kill y' all… this o'le boy surely will…"

Walter, rose, pointing his instrument of death at Harley's sweating forehead. Retreating backwards Harley blared, "Ya… som bitch… how ya knows me?"

"You… you… why Harley your exploits are knowed world-wide. Yessir, world-wide."

All eyes were focused on the two central figures in the unfolding drama.

"Harley… boy. It's me… 'Durango'. Dontcha know me?"

Harley began to move this right arm behind him… toward the waiting .36 Cal. navy colt… hidden beneath his jacket as he spat, "Not wid dat… hood on ya face… niggar."

Walter seemed no to notice the Calvary man's move… while holding his .44 leveled at Gibb's forehead. Harley's next move was quick, he pulled his weapon… with speed… got it waist high and… Now Harley's daddy, Whitmore Struck Gibbs, had always taught his son that a white man was better 'n a "niggar"… any day. It were <u>every</u> white man's sworn duty, ta be shore ta keep "niggars" in dey' 'God appointed places'… at da bottom.

Intelligence and understanding did not run 'amock' in the Gibbs family… neither did truth… justice… or common sense. If they had Harley might have lived longer… they did not… he did not…

'Durango' fired… sending a .44 Cal. slug into Harley Gibb's face. Harley's next move was quicker than his first. He dropped the Colt, screamed, flung his hands toward what was left of his face… Took one… no… two steps backward, hit the hot Texas soil and… died!

Military veteran Sergeant Bill Nary was brave… he had the medals to prove it… but he wasn't… stupid. He 'ordered' the remaining members of his detail to sit perfectly… still! Walter, stepping over the dead trooper, moved toward the wagon and asked, respectfully, for the Fort Walker… payroll… all $30,000 of it. He only had to ask… once!

Civilians Haskall and Evans almost collided, in their rush, to hand over the Army's loot. The U.S. Cavalry payed well for their services… very well… but not well enough ta… die.

Jackson ordered the civilians to exit the wagon, opposite the box containing the money, 'n strip ta 'What God gave 'um,' lying face down.

The troopers came next. They were 'requested' to do the same, one at a time.

'Durango' collected the weapons and placed them in the wagon. He collected the clothes and… sat them on fire. He collected a rope from the wagon, tied the men together 'n spooked the mules inta flight. He collected his horse… collected his gang… and they collectively rode off in the direction of Coopersville… leavin the two troopers, Sgt. Nary, and the two civilians… collectively… 'cussin'… their… collective… souls.

Novell Jecter sat inside Cage's Feed 'N seed damn near drunk… stinkin more than usual. Thanks, in part to the heat and because he had not washed in two weeks.

He sat… alone… the fumes from last night's bout with diarrhea greatly benefiting his 'dearth' of companionship. It was nearing 9 p.m. Feeling sullen, Jecter were askin himself, Whar was Harley? Whar was da troopers? Whar was da 'niggar' 'n da res o' de gang?

He was goin down ta da Smithy's few a look 'n see. It was whar he 'n Harley was gonna lure Jackson 'n kill him fer da… rewards. Dey was gonna ask fer help wid da res 'of da gang… Pete Cage was most glad to see the treacherous and stinking man leave… They would meet later tonight for Cage's share of the Army payroll… Pete began to sweat… he could already feel Big Mable's wet lips on his organ of manhood…

Mable Oaks was… big. She was a whore, excuse me, a "good" whore. She was… three-way; oral, anal, and vaginal. She was basically… hygienic. Not unusual for someone in her profession. Evenso, she knew from past experience that within the next two weeks, some of her 'clients' would come down with a rip-roaring case of… drips (Gonorrhea). 'Ya pays ya money 'n ya takes ya chances.'

Sure, she made Harley pay for access to the prize she carried between… her legs. What 'honorable' working girl wouldn't? No matter, Mable truly loved U.S. Cavalry trooper Harley Gibbs! Harley had confided they would kill the outlaw… 'Durango'… his gang… 'n… Pete Cage!

Even in the dark, damn near drunk, and… stinkin… Novell Jecter 'knew' who the figure was standing just inside the Black Smith's Shop. Novell's clearing head coincided with the click of the six-gun aimed at him. "Grab some sky… Jecter," the voice commanded, Novell did not have to be told… twice. 'Durango' then ordered the 'odorous' man up the steps to the loft… "Why ya bees turning on me Mista Jackson?"

"A dollar but a lot… a hundred dollars a lot… more!" Jecter spun around in a 'rage', loudly protesting his innocence. "Da fat bitch be a lyin… I were no parts a naw plans to do ya murda fer naw rewards. Mista Jackson… Jecter was unable to finish his statement. 'Durango' brought the barrel of his .44-.40 across the man's head, sending him into oblivion.

As the early morning sun began to streak the sky, Novell Jecter awoke with a splitting headache, a blood-stained face, his hands and feet tied and a rope around his neck.

"Puleez suh, Mista Jackson… O'l Novell he knows ya… puleez!"

"Familiarity… breeds contempt… you stinkin bastard." Jackson pushed Jecter from the loft… breaking… his unwashed neck. There swung Novell… still damn near drunk… still stinkin… still… dead… still.

While Novell Jecter was having his 'ill-fated' meeting with… eternity, Mable Oaks was applying a sweet smelling powder to the mountainous globes that served as breasts.

Pete Cage, who already had an erection, was finishing up his late night wash-up.

Col. Daily Ransom Walker was just about… there. There being drunk enough to make love to his 'homely' wife as the wall clock stuck 11 p.m.

Interestingly enough, Molly Fair Walker waited… patiently… for her drunk of a… husband… to stumble into bed. Some love was better than <u>no</u> love… wasn't it?

He was dead, no… not dead… now Harley he… was… dead!

Sgt. Bill Nary was 'dead' tired as he and his 'motley' crew sighted the outskirts of Coopersville.

Their impending arrival created quite a stir. Constable Cause Walters moved, as fast as his aging body would allow, toward the Fort Walker Detail.

The commotion 'forced' Pete Cage to forget… momentarily… his erection… as he ran out into what served as Main Street, joining a few 'late-night townies'.

The commotion interrupted Mable Oaks' final act of getting dressed. She squatted to swab out her "koochie pie" one final time. "Her second set of… lips"… parted on their own. She dropped the wet cloth into the bath water, pulled down her dress… she <u>never</u> wore underpants on a date… and rushed to join the excitement on Main Street.

Bill Nary leaned forward on his mount, hoping the gesture made him 'look' official. It took near two hours… and… then some to catch dem… damn mules. Luck had it… there was a box of brand new Army Issues on board… being sent back to Washington for proper stitchin… or 'ol Bill 'n da boys would be addressin da crowd… naked.

The late night crowd of… six… listened intently as Constable Walters said, "What be wrong Bill? Needin ma help?"

"Naw Constable, naw needs fer help… now."

"As Sergeant O'dis Har detail it is mah sad 'n solemen duty, ta tells ya da payroll been robed… all $30,000… o' it. The sergeant continued, "Taken by some vicos (vicious) 'hooded' highwaymen. One man kilt." An uneasy calm fell over the 'capacity' crowd, "Trooper Harley Gibbs."

The calm was violated by a scream, which erupted from Mable Oaks' throat. Folks say it was louder… and lasted longer… than that of Mrs. Olsaski's the night Mr. Olsaski missed her vagina and hit her anus in raucous celebration of their twenty-fifth wedding anniversary.

The bards say 'Hell hath no fury like a woman scorned'. In Coopersville, "Hell hath no fury like a 'big woman' when she learns the man she loves has… been… killed."

And, Harley had been… killed.

Big Mable was amazingly quick for her size. She tore through the sparse crowd past Bill Nary's mount, and… grabbed… the throat of the man she knew(?) had betrayed her… and… her… dead lover!

Pete had 'wrestled' with Mable many times… but… never when she had him in a 'death' grip. Mable's unexpected move and the ensuing fireworks caught the non-combatants by… surprise. Pete grabbed his bowie knife and began flailing away. Pete flailed… Mable wailed… and… revealed much about their ill-fated plan.

Big Mable would die late the next day, just about the time a soon-to-be retired Bill Nary and his detail arrived at Fort Samuel T. Walker.

Minus the payroll… minus Harley Gibbls. But, Nary and his crew had all the supplies the Quartermaster ordered. They had Pete Cage for aiding in the selling of a government payroll schedule… and… murder!

Col. Daily Ransom Walker had… a… hangover. Molly Fair Walker had… had… a 'welcomed' night of… love making.

The Jackson Gang had… the Fort Walker payroll… all $30,000… and they had made a successful get away… for… now!

The Exodusters
The Man From Texas

CHAPTER SIX

Leaving the stinking Jecter 'hangin' 'Durango' met his companions near the outskirts of Coopersville.

Without words they rode to their hideout. To the surprise of Bound and Doolittle, the old man had everything packed… and ready to go!

"We quittin the territory Walter?" A shocked Ham asked. "Yeah, be goin to Montana. I got a small spread there… a few hundred acres… few hundred head. My cut from this haul will pay the place off. Matthew will go by train. We'll be followin… on horseback… looking for the Army 'n 'Johnny Law'.

"It's time we quit outlawin 'n become honest men… "gentlemen ranchers."

"Just what we need ta do… quit robbin 'n go ta nursemaidin cows," was Ham's retort.

This was the second time, in the same day, Walter had 'surprised' his old friend… Sever Bound, who smiled and thought about their 'new' lives… as "gentlemen ranchers"… in a… 'new' land.

The 'reformed' Jackson Gang was off to… Montana!

Close to the time Walter was galloping onto a 'new' trail in his life, she… she being Grea Merced… was helping her father put away the hymnals of the Prism Creek Baptist Church. The Rev. Horticie Merced did not, would not, would never, approve of his daughter's 'sinful' relationship… with the notorious gunman… 'Durango'.

He did not have to look at her to know her thoughts… and her heart… were… with… him!

Rev. Merced knew his daughter did not give her heart, or anything else away… at the 'drop of a hat'…

Maybe it was the night scent of pine, or the fresh breeze blowing through the choir stand's window, which made her think about… their 'first time'… the first time he had… penetrated… her.

It had happened… outside… on the deck of the Riverboat Corina. They… she… and the ladies of the Church who could afford passage, were traveling to St. Louis. They were meeting a shipment of bibles and choir robes… from back East.

Lunch with the man from Texas, known as "Durango', had been filled with laughter and 'light' conversation. Later dinner, dancing and 'direct' conversation. A moon-lit walk to the upper deck of the Corina… his hand touched her cheek… a passionate embrace… a deep kiss… When he entered her, her thighs had… "trembled"

She became 'wet' each time she recalled that 'wonderful'… night!

Grea did not know where 'Durango' was… but… wherever it… was… she was determined… to join him.

Grea loved Walter and he loved… her.

Even if… he… wouldn't admit… it!

Nick Jones

CHAPTER SEVEN

Matthew Tagon looked on while Ramos Wade, the hostler from Coopersville, drove away from the BBD&Q Waterstop west of town.

Tagon had made arrangements to sell the wagon, after Walter told him "to get packed." Once the contents were loaded… he did just that. He even turned a 'small' profit.

Matthew was the only passenger boarding. He moved toward the train when the conductor yelled, "We're leavin… Mister."

Watching the 'violent' Texas country side drift into the background, Matthew felt good about their 'Exodus' to Montana… slumping to take a nap, his hand curled around the butt of his .36 Cal. Navy Colt…

Nick Jones

CHAPTER EIGHT

The Llano Estacado had been good to the Antelopes (Quahdi). Moon Dog, Running Cow, Screaming Elk and Dark River were returning with much contraband. The successful raid would make Moon Dog a… Chief… he would bargain for the hand of the lovely 'She Who Does Not See Well'.

His friend, Running Cow, had agreed to approach the tepee of 'He Who's Kinfe Drips With Blood', 'She Who Does Not See Well's' father.

With Running Cow's two horses and his four… Moon Dog knew 'She Who Does Not See Well'… would be his!

When the time arrived for Running cow to chose a Quahadi (Antelope) maiden, probably 'Stone Belly', Moon Dog would do the same for him.

The near naked warriors rode proudly through their land… now infested with the 'hated' white man… and the disease and destruction his coming had brought… to Antelope territory. But… the white man's number had been reduced! Moon Dog's band had raided… twice. The farm house… The Calvary patrol. 'Wolf That Howls', 'Racing Turtle', 'Fat Bird', and 'Deer Without Horns' had been killed… each had fought fiercely and each had… died… Well. 'Dark River' had been badly wounded, but rode without complaint, as the band neared the Antelope's summer camp.

Their horses easily began to climb a small rise. 'Moon Dog' thought, with disdain, of the cowardly way the 'stupid' white man fought. With eight

Antelope warriors, he… he… had conquered a force of thirty adults… and six children.

All lay dead, Each had suffered a 'fate' learned from the white man… they had been… scalped!

Their remains lay, rotting, in the hot east Texas sun, awaiting the arrival of the 'DU-KAF-TOW-U' (The Buzzards).

The farm house and the remaining possessions of the 'misfortunate' settlers were nothing but a… pile… of ashes. The pony soldiers had been made to… suffer!

For Moon Dog and his Quahadi Band… it had been a very good… day!

For Sam Acker, his wife Ari, and their six children: Samuel Jr., Ruth, Bradford, Ronald, Kathy, and Baby Lile… it had been a 'bad' day, a very… bad… day.

Before dying… Sam were a-thankin maybe… they dun shoulda stay in Ohio…

For the fifteen Fort Ruther-Ford B. Hayes Troopers; four Indian scouts; two newspaper men and the minister from Flat Head Pass it had been worse… much… much… worse!

CHAPTER NINE

"When we get near the top o' that lil' hill, we'll take us a breather." Walter's cinch slipped. He reigned abruptly causing Sever, who was directly behind him, to veer sharply to the right. Walter dismounted, Sever pulled along side.

Ham found the incident 'humorous', saying, "Ya gals havin trouble playin folla-the-leader? I'll have a go at it."

Jackson, perplexed that he had failed to properly secure an essential piece of his equipment, did it portend of darker things?, said, "Suit ya self"

Ham Doolilttle seemed happier than a 'pig saved from slaughter' to ride out front… he turned and said, "Sure feels good to be… alive."

As he turned his attention to the trail ahead… his heart hung in mid-beat… Screaming Elk's arrow thumped into his chest, exited his back, and… killed him. Before the dead outlaw's body fell to earth, Walter had swung into the saddle. Jackson and Bound raced off with Moon Dog's bunch in hot pursuit. For awhile it seemed the harder Walter and Sever rode… the closer the Quahadi got.

The outlaws hit a dry wash on the fly, glancing at each other, spun and fired a volley into the on-rushing Antelopes. The abrupt move caught the Comanches by surprise. It surprised Running Cow more… the fire and lead hurled into "He Who's Knife Drips With Bloods' Warriors, tore off Running Cow's… head. Dismounting and using their horses as shields, Moon

Dog, Dark River and Screaming Elk sought cover behind… whatever they could find.

Watching the surviving Antelopes take shelter, Walter and Sever realized their mixed… blessing. The wash provided adequate protection… only one way in… but… only one way out! To leave the 'reformed' outlaws would have to expose themselves to the waiting Quahadi. They could wait until dark and perhaps, somehow, slip past the Antelopes. What if this group were not afraid o' night fightin? Every male Quahadi (Comanche) was a warrior, bought up to believe in courage and bravery… they fought to the death… they had no fear of the dead!

Comanches are said to have believed after death they went to Heaven, with the exception of those scalped after death or were strangled, died in the dark or were mutilated.

Firing his weapon, Sever shouted, "Figure these here fellas gonna fight us tonight?" Watching the skyline, Walter replied, "Don't know… we best get out… while we kin!" Considering that there was not much to hide behind, the Antelopes were a-doin a bang up job.

"Sever, see that one over there ta the left… the one on the end!"

"Yeah"

"Aim fer his legs… it's the only thing we might be able to get a clear shot at."

At first, Moon Dog, Screaming Elk and Dark River thought the two white men (?) were 'bad' shots… until Moon Dog felt the searing lead pierce his lower legs and upper buttocks, causing him to raise, momentarily in pain…

It was long enough for Walter to send a .44-.40 slug smashin inta the side o' his skull.

The dying Moon Dog was covered in his own gore… of brains, blood and, shattered bone… a brief exchange of gunfire and then… silence… silence.

The sun drifted slowly into the western horizon. Walter checked his pocket watch, perhaps out of habit, it was 7:30 p.m… 7:30 p.m… just this side of… Hell!

Not one shot had been fired in over three or, was it four hours… and, no one had moved.

"Sever, if the markins I saw on them Comanches out yonder was correct… they should be Antelopes."

"Didn't get that good a look Walter… what difference would it be makin?"

"They believe in Heaven just… like us… but, not if their dead been violated. I'm gonna head out 'n strangle that one we shot in the legs… should draw the last two… out!"

"Walter… you gonna strangle a… dead… man? Now that there sure is a violation! How will that be keeping us alive? What do you want from me? What it be not… Antelopes?"

"Guess I'll be doin all this here work… fer… nothing. My friend, when you get a shot… don't… miss!"

Removing the .44-.40 from his front holster and, using what sparse cover there was, Jackson moved slowly toward the… dead Quahadi. Dark River and Screaming Elk heard the rustling in the weeds but, could not and, would not, move…

To do so would mean… death… from the white men's long guns. Were the 'BO-TA-KAS' (white men) working to surround them? Would the one who killed Moon Dog… come first? Would they both strike at the same time? Dark River had five shells left… which direction? Five bullets… what could be worse?

What was worse came gallopin outa the night… assaulting his senses, causing his blood to run cold… There, framed by matchlight, was Moon dog… with the white man's (?) belt around his neck… strangling his… spirit.

Fear, revulsion and courage, all caused Dark River to charge toward his fallen comrade. He did… firing rapidly… exposing himself. Some say you never hear the bullet that… kills… you. Dark River 'heard' the bark from Sever Bound's long gun. As life's final darkness enveloped him, Dark River wondered if the white man (?) who strangled Moon Dog… would strangle him… now that he was… dead! Screaming Elik's end was less dramatic… but… just as… final! He, as had the ill-fated Dark River charged, he charged a twirling 'Durango', still clutching the dead… and now strangled… Moon Dog, Screaming Elk's aim was true! The bullet from his .50 Cal. Sharps hit an unknowing Moon Dog just below the heart, exited his back and stopped… just above 'Durango's' third rib… with a thud! Flat on his back, fighting immense pain and unconsciousness, Walter snapped off three shots… separating Screaming Elk from this rifle… and his… life!

For 'Durango', shot and damn near out, it was a hellava beginning of his trip to Montana… the "Promised Land!"

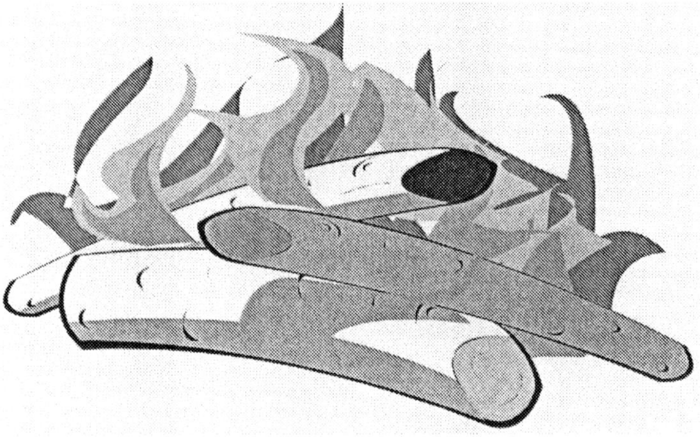

CHAPTER TEN

Local folks said it were warm for this time o' year in Augusta Ridge, Montana. Eight long months had passed. Evenso, he sat in the sun wrapped in a blanket.

The trek to the ranch had… been… Hell!

The doctor said he was, that is now, healing… fine. At first, it had been touch and go… with more lean toward the 'goin'.

Walter Thomas Jackson should be 'proud' of himself! He was 'sure' his grandparents would have been. They had raised him.

He dun went from choirboy… to… professional gunman!

He was the best!

He was recovering from a gunshot wound!

He was… still… a WANTED man!

And now, he could never show his face… again… on the Texas/Oklahoma border!

He had… killed… he would… kill… again!

How many were it… now?

Sometimes he could still see their… death… faces.

Sometimes he could still hear their… death… screams.

Sometimes he could still smell their… death… smells.

Why were it be Ham bees kilt and not… he?

He was the best!

There had always been… women. Lot o' dem!

Now there were… Grea.

Still… inside he felt… empty.

Perhaps... perhaps... problem be he had dun buried parts o' his... heart... wid ever man he had... kilt!

It bees hard ta know... love... when ya only dealin... pain!

He was the best!

But... why was he cryin... inside?

He was the best!

Nick Jones

CHAPTER ELEVEN

The weather was not a concern. Rain, shine, or snow, it felt good to be on a horse again. It felt good to be… alive!

God had, indeed, smiled on Augusta Ridge, Montana. It was a place of beauty… especially to a ‘reformed’ outlaw and a ‘reformed’, hopefully, gunman.

Walter and an “investor” in the /J (Slash J) Ranch were ridin the line… checking their cattle, their fences and, their water on the small two-hundred acre spread.

It was hard, sunup to sundown, work. They accomplished this difficult task with the help of four others and… Matthew Tagon.

For Walter Jackson and Sever Bound, ranchin was ‘one helluva jollification’, compared to outlawin. Honest men didn’t get shot at… at least… not as much as… outlaws… and gunmen… Could be they both wondered why it had taken them so… long… to recognize the difference!

If they did wonder, neither would ever admit it to the other… they were ‘enjoyin’ the work, the sweat, the landscape, the not getting shot at… at least… not in the last year and a half.

Yessir, this was ‘one helluva jollification!’

Drainin the last drops of his beer, W. Walker Williams slid the glass onto the table… and smiled. He had, or thought he had, heard jest ‘bout… everything… until… today! In his thirty years plus o’ working as a Paid Assassin, he had heard, seen, or done 'bout all ta be dod!

Even got so drunk, once, in Matamosa, Mexico he had… "let" a Mexican whore suck his male member… while she was being 'impaled' from… behind… by a… donkey.

What a night!

W.W. was 'sore' in his 'personals' for a week! That, he would admit, was wild! W.W. had been offered mucho dinero' to do a… killin. But, what was a-bein offered… now… well, it were what a 'sane' man would call… crazy!

No matter, in the killin business, an "astute entrepreneur" never turned down… a… dolla. Sho'nuf. 'N Dis Har… Har… was some big dollars. Ma'bees a mite… too… much? Passing the stack of bills toward the 'renowned' murderer, he person asked, "When can you leave?"

"Tonite", was Walker's response. "Be a takin… 'n dat dar… bauble… ta seal ourn 'greement'!"

His 'smiling' patron produced a bottle of "Good" store bought whiskey… filling a glass for… himself… and filling W.W.'s beer mug to the… brim.

The Exodusters
The Man From Texas

CHAPTER TWELVE

They had seen him ambling along for the last mile… or… so. And why not, he… the rider… made no effort to 'conceal' himself.

'Jack' Hayes Ward scratched hisself, stretched, 'passed-gas', and handed the bottle of whiskey to fella… killa… 'n drankin buddy… Stubblefield Smith.

"Got me two dolbies har says I know who it be," Ward said. Feeling 'generous', perhaps because he was half drunk, Smith answered, "Bet ta ya. Who it be?"

"Bees Ole W.W," Ward replied. A doubting Smith asked, "Thought he be mo' a city fella. Wonda what brangs him disaways?"

As Williams neared his 'Bucolic' associates, he nodded saying, "Where's Grant?"

"Behind ya sodbusta, now drop them hoglegs o' yourn," was a smiling Grant Minor's reply.

Turning slowly, W. Walker Williams faced his second-in-command. What they 'commanded' was <u>one</u> of the world's worst collection of backshooters, liars, cheats, cattle 'n hoss thieves ever gathered at 'a supper table'.

As evil as Terry Sun, Booker Bert, who were both asleep because they had worked the nightshift… stealing… cattle, 'Jack' Hayes Ward, and Stubblefield Smith <u>were</u>… they were <u>less</u> then 'spit on a prairie fire', compared to… Grant Minor… and… W. Walker Williams.

The tie that bound this 'pernicious' group together was money… nuthin more… nutin less! Williams was… fast… but for what he had been paid to do… he was gonna be a needin… help!

… And those who were, unknowingly, about to be visited by W. Walker Williams… 'n friends… was… a gonna be a needin… help!

Nick Jones

CHAPTER THIRTEEN

He stood facing his small, but growing congregation, he felt the need to make his announcement… immediately!

"Church… as the good book says in Exodus, Chapter 17, verse 1…

"'We must set out on our journey from the wilderness of sin'… Truly church… there is no water for the people to drink…"

The most Reverend Merced was… right. The county court's battle with the state over who owned the water rights to the land where Prism Creek Baptist Church was located… was… a… problem!

It was, however, a larger problem for the ranchers and farmers… Their Exodus would come only as a result of… blood… being… shed.

The recent influx of 'whores', 'killers', and 'thieves' had no doubt motivated Rev. Horticie Merced to leave… the once peaceful… town of Miracle Valley, Texas.

He had never planned to… leave. With the 'Exodus' of the 'vicious' Jackson Gang. Knothole County had begun to shape us as… the place to be! His daughter would have the 'opportunity' to marry… a… 'decent man…

And now this, the 'war' for something God had placed on His earth to be shared by all His creatures… water!

The result, more plague and pestilence… in the form of 'faceless' killers, 'nameless' thieves, and 'countless' whores…

Regardless, Rev. Merced took a deep breath and said, "We are leaving this land of 'sin', looking into the beautiful face of his… only… child, we are going to Montana."

Grea could hardly contain her joy. Her father had said… Montana! Montana… Walter… the man she loved more than life itself? The Reverend continued, "In Montana, in Horseheads Creek, Montana there is land to be bought. Land to be tilled. Families to be raised. A Church… to be… Built."

The 'good' Reverend knew he could count on the the Cooper and Nelsen families… He would have to 'sell' the rest of the congregation. Rev. Merced 'knew' they would be "jumpy about exchanging a devil they 'knew' for an angel… they did not… know!"

No matter, he had a purpose. He had vision. He had… some… of his congregation. And, he… had… his daughter's smile… again!

The Exodusters
The Man From Texas

CHAPTER FOURTEEN

Dawn broke through the cabin window with the explosiveness of a .44-.40 and the beauty of a new born child!

As time passed, Matthew Tagon had grown to appreciate the way… God… blessed… this land. It was one hellava turn around for an 'ex-gunman' and the leader of one of Texas' most bloodied gangs. Maybe… it were old age… maybe it were the Priest over at Mooselick. Matthew… taken ta reading the Good Book. Thinkin about… God!

Maybe… it were a lots of things… maybe.

Matthew stoked his cook fire. That was another change he had made. He was still a 'fair' hand with… a… gun. But, hardly toted one anymore. He had become a better than 'fair' cook. With <u>all</u> the hands out on the range, he headed for the stream to get… water… for the stew he was afixin fer the sundown meal. The stream water made his stews and soups taste… 'better'… then the water from the well. He thought about taking his "trusted" .36 Cal. Navy Colt. But then decided against it. Grabbed two water buckets and headed for the… stream!

What a beautiful morning in Augusta Ridge. The Ranch was shaping up ta be some outfit! Droppin his buskets, Matthew knelt and drank the cold-sweet water form this 'special' stream… Try as he may, he jes' didn't 'member the water tastin this salty… 'afore… Matthew plunged into the 'special' stream's waiting arms… spilling blood… and wearing a sickening red-black looking hole… where the back of his… neck… had once… been. Matthew Tagon's life… slipped… away.

"Ta-wernt a bad bits-a-work, were it?" asked 'Jack' Ward, as he, smilingly, took the burned blanket off his long gun. The blanket had been used to muffle the Henry Carbine's roar. "Naw, it twer not," said Subblefield Smith.

They eased toward the floating, mortal, remains of the 'reformed outlaw'… and… crudely fired four more shots into his… lifeless… body…

Near the time Matthew Tagon's mortality was… slipping… away, Walter's was, at least a good dosage, entering the still withering Junellen Kaye. Ms. Kaye, who's supple thighs were wrapped around 'Durango's' upper torso tighter that a Sears catalog corset, took her 'come' three times before she allowed the willingly 'entrapped' outlaw… his… momentary freedom!

They then laid in each others arms, without speaking, touching… cooing… kissing… igniting their passion… once… again!

Later, after washing each other thoroughly in Junellen's bath tub… they sat on the porch sipping flavored brandy. Enthralled by the view of the distant hills.

"Walter," she said. "Yes," he answered. "Do you… care for me as much as you do… Grea?" Without hesitation he responded, "I do if you believe a man can 'care' for two women… equally… but in different ways."

"Does she make you… feel…"

He interrupted her before she completed he query. "Darlin… you are like a blazin star to this cowboy's lonely night… but… please don't press me on ma feeling fer either of ya"!

Junellen sat, silently, for an undetermined amount of time. When she spoke, it was with the 'authority' of a U.S. Calvary 10=barrel, crank revolved, gatling gun with the 400 theoretical shots-a-minute… stricking 'Durango'… between the eyes. "Walter, I love you!"

"Yes, Junellen, I kinda… felt… ya… did.

They each returned to the most private recesses of their separate but equal feelings!

Reality came flooding back with a rush, for him moreso than her, along with Sheriff Hope Dungraver's approaching horse.

Bringing back, for him, that eerie feeling and that tenseness in his belly. That eerie feeling and that tension 'Durango' had not felt since he had… killed… his last man. That… Quahadi before leavin Texas.

Texas, a damn good place ta be… away… from!

CHAPTER FIFTEEN

"Evenin, Ms. Junellen. Ya Aunt Melody in?"

"No… she is not Sheriff. She went over to Mooselick. She made some tapestry for the Parish and took them to Father Josua. They both wanted them hung in time for Sunday's Mass."

Church talk. All of this was lost on… 'Durango'… who had not been inside a church in so long… he had been advised that if (?) he ever went again… 'ta be shore ta knock 'afore enterin?' "Sounds rite fine, mamam," was Sheriff Dungraver's reply.

Turning his attention to the silent outlaw/rancher, Dungraver said, "Ya best be a comin wid me… Walter. Been a… killin… at ya spread. Knowed ya'd want ta hear 'bout rite aways."

Sitting forward and staring hard Walter asked, "Who… dun had they toes turned ta the daisies?"

"Get ya hoss, we bees a talking on da way. Ya gonna be alrite Ms. Junellen?," the Sheriff responded.

No stranger to the 'frontier's equalizer', Junellen said, "Yes sir, Sheriff. My Aunt is due back any time… and Chief "Man Who Walks Backwards' braves are camped down in the Meadow… Junellen's widowed Aunt Melody Hart and moved into the territory of Arizona in the '60's with her husband, then a Corporal. Jebudiah 'Sure-Shot' Hart of the honorable 10th U.S. Calvalry. Life for a cavalryman's wife was bleak, hard, lonely and further complicated because <u>not</u> <u>every</u> Arizonian 'appreciated' their lives, families, and <u>property</u> being protected by a bunch of 'brunettes'. The term that was, often, used in public. In private the toopers and their families were often called... 'niggers'

Nonetheless, the 'fightin tenth' served honorably... and with distinction!

'Sure-Hot' and Melody had been one of the... first... black families in Augusta Ridge. With his retirement pay, the money she had taken in from 'washing' and their savings... Jebudiah bought the farm with the rich black soil for growing things. Unfortunately... children... would never sprout in this... fertile... ground!

Years fightin the "A-pach' (Apache) in the acidulous Arizona wastelands and, an Apache arrow in his lower back, had 'taught' Jebudiah to... at least try to live with... the Red Man!

Therefore, upon arriving, although he held the title, Jebudiah acknowledged it was the Crow Tribe who owned the land. He and Crow Chief 'Man Who Walks Backwards' had struck a 'deal'... live and... let live...

It was not uncommon ta find 'signs' anywhere on the Hart place... when Jebudiah died doing one of the things he loved in life, although, in his late seventies, breaking a new colt 'Man Who Walks Backwards' continued to serve as... a... friend! and a protector!

So, Junellen was safe... quite safe... but, that had not always been... true!

Watching the Sheriff and the man she loved ride toward the Ranch, a sudden gust of cold mountain air brought back memories of her long 'dead' past... bad... memories...

The ride from Crane Neck, Mississippi to St. Louis, Missouri in Lyle and Sara Webster's wagon had been everything she thought it would be! Hot, sweaty, dirty, short rations, and mid-way… her cycle… had started. It wasn't due for two weeks.

Fortunately, there were several other women, at twenty-five 'dollars-a-head', crammed into the rolling pigsty. So, Junellen <u>found</u> the 'absorption materials' she… needed.

Arrival in St. Louis meant a quick trip to a hotel, a comfortable room and then pure 'pleasure'… a… hot… hot… bath! It was needed, she… stank!

Three 'restful' days later, in both mind and spirit, Junellen's trip from St. Louis to Chicago, by train, was everything she had hoped it would be! <u>Comfortable</u>.

Junellen could barely restrain her glee when she was met at the train station by the most beautiful carriage she had ever… seen.

It was driven by a most elegantly dressed black coachmen. He carried her 'ratty' looking suitcase, took her hand and, assisted Junellen into the carriage's cushiony seat…

The ride to Aunt Lue's seemed to erase the 'bad' images of the first half of the journey. Aunt Lue's cobblestone, that is Louise Ann Sibonie's cobblestone, was (?) as big as the Osmothis Plantation Junellen had… left… in Mississippi. But, this city… this Chicago… was lovely. All these people. She was going to 'love'… it here!

Along with the morning sun, her Aunt's smile, a <u>hot</u> tray brought 'country' breakfast, Junellen began her, 'unknowing', decent… into… Hell!

Hell… was learning that her 'favorite' Aunt Lue was a fine brown combination owner/whore/manager of one of Chicago's biggest, and the best Lue said, gambling/whorehouse/eateries… for colored folk.

And, a lot of what was 'ate' wasn't… fried… chicken!

Hell… was learning to deal Faro, from the bottom of the deck, the House… won… when it had to!

Hell… was selling watered down 'rot-gut', to intoxicated customers, at exorbitant prices.

Hell… was being told she would do these things. All things her, now dead parents had raised her not to do! Or… be put out… on the Chicago streets!

Hell… was having to 'sell' herself… on 'several' occasions… Three years later, Junellen saw a 'knowing' way out of… Hell'.

Aunt Lue, whom Junellen wished would go to… Hell… had sent a maid to tell Junellen she was wanted in Lue's upstairs office.

Junellen had been helping to prepare food for the soon to be arriving customers. "Junellen Mable Kay, I have a 'special' customer I want you… to… meet. He's due within the hour. Take this… I should deliver… it… myself. But I must attend Alderman Karshonski's… 'needs'. Now, go and come right… back! You must get properly dressed…"

"Yes Mamam." Junellen went down and opened the front door. Walked down the steps of the fashionable cobblestone on Chicago's lower east side. Her hair was in braids and she was barefoot. The bribe money for the local Chicago constabulary was under her arm… it was as if the Lord was saying go. So, Junellen Kay just… went.

As dust drifted into the stage coach's window, Junellen said a silent prayer of thanks. She had escaped Aunt Lue and the hell-hole of Chicago's 'colored' underworld with her life… if… not… her virtue! Junellen was headed to an 'unknowing', Aunt Melody in… Montana!…

As the night shadows rode across the sky, she reentered her not… vacant… bedroom. Lighting the candle on the nightstand… reminded her of how she had met… the man from Texas.

It was near a year-or so after 'Durango' had been… shot… by the Comanche Brave leaving… Texas! It had happened, quite innocently, in of all places the… Parish… at Mooselick.

She had been… lighting a candle… for the repose of the… soul… of her Uncle and other family, who had crossed… over!

As she had turned to blow out the match and pray at the alter, she noticed the… man. No, the handsome… man seated in the rear of the church. The man… staring straight ahead… at… nothing. That's how they had come to be!

Her mind bounced back to the present, with a… jolt. Who had been killed at the J- Ranch? A question she could not answer. An answer she could not question was she 'knew' she had fallen… for the man from… Texas!

She 'knew' her heart was… his. Just as surely as water was… wet. <u>All</u> her life she had <u>had</u> to… fight… for anything and everything…

She would… fight… Grea or anyone else for the man from… Texas.

Junellen's tears seemed to be in 'rhythm' with the melting wax sliding down her bedroom… candle.

Nick Jones

CHAPTER SIXTEEN

As Walter and Hope Dungraver approached the rise leading to the Ranch, that eerie feeling and tenseness in the belly jumped up a notch… for… 'Durango'!

The corpse had been covered with a piece of canvas, the small gathering moved aside allowing 'Durango' and Sheriff Dungraver to pass.

Micah Nelson, the range foreman was the first to speak, "It bees… Matthew… boss. It bees Matthew Tagon"!

Without a word, Walter dismounted, peeled back the canvas… and just… stared! Moments, which seemed like hours, loped by but… there was no response from… the man from Texas. Witnesses say Walter Jackson spoke very clearly that… terrible… day. He spoke with… his… eyes. His eyes had said somebody was gonna die fer this. Somebody was gonna die… hard!… The funeral mass had been performed by the Priest over at Mooselick. Father Josua Thomas, who prayed… and prayed well, for the repose of the soul of… Matthew Tagon.

It was to him, several days later, 'Durango' spoke, "not a bad meal… fer a… Padre. But, why the invite?"

The quiet man of God, with the sad eyes, slowly said, "I have not always been a… Priest."

"Figured as much," Walter replied. 'Durango' continued, "No man falls inta this here, if ya pardon me Father, 'Veil of Tears', jes as he bees when ya first… meets! I recon ya dun a thing or two other than padrayin." Taking a sip of the delicious wine from the parish's vineyard, Father Josua's response was "Yes... Mr. Jackson, many... things. No matter, it is... you... I wish to talk about."

The man of the cloth's curt retort caused 'Durango' to eye the Priest, momentarily, as... an... adversary. A worthy adversary! "Aint much ta tell... Padre. Jes a po' black man up from Texas... a tryin ta make a 'go' in a-way-farin land," Walter's tongue-in-cheek reply.

Depositing another piece of cheese in his mouth and, washing it down with the 'sweet' wine, it was the priest... staring hard... who laid open the gateway to Walter's past.

"How long are you going to try 'n cat and mouse most of the folk here in Augusta Ridge... 'Durango'?," Father Josua asked. Damn... here we go again, 'Durango' thought. As that eerie feeling and the tenseness in his belly... smashed... the gate of the 'mental' corral Walter... 'hoped'... would hold!

Collecting himself, 'Durango' shot the Padre a glance that would have melted a bar of lead. Slowly, the man who <u>had</u> thought he could outride his past, spoke. "Sir, I have always readied myself fer... any sit'cheation. 'Pears ta me, I shore got me one... here! Who else... knows?"

"Myself, Sheriff Dungraver, Mayor Talbert and Territorial Judge Osco Mead up at the Capitol in Horsehead's Creek."

'Durango' asked, "how? And... whatcha planning ta do?"

Father Josua, sinking back into his chair and lighing his pipe, replied, "A letter with an Arizona wanted dodger arrived almost a week ago… for me. I don't know when or… how… the others were informed."

"Then how do ya know the others… know?"

The Priest began, "In a… should I call you Walter or… should I call you 'Durango'?" the outlaw/rancher's answer was, "Which ever keeps ya hammer tied down!"

"As I was saying", Father Josua Thomas continued, "the Sheriff received a wire from Judge Mead. He shared that information with the Mayor, the Sheriff and I discussed the matter after… Mr. Tagon's… funeral. To my knowledge, Walter Jackson is the man who owns the J- Ranch. I don't know 'Durango'… and… from what I've heard, I don't… care to!"

rolling and then lighting his 'quirly', Walter said, "most… don't!"

"If I may continue… Walter. You've broken no laws in… Montana. The killing of Mr. Tagon concerns us… all. We just want the… law… to handle this matter. For there not to be any… more… killings! Are you Catholic… Walter?"

"Yes… I was baptized inta the… faith."

Taking a deep breath the Priest looked the man from Texas in the eye and said, "Vengeance is mine sayeth the Lord. Please remember… that for your good… and the good of our community."

"Father, with all due respect to… God… ya self, and the community, I'm gonna be lendin… God… a 'hand' in this here deal. Walter rose and walked out of Father Josua Thomas's quarters. The Priest, with the sad eyes, entered the Chapel and knelt before the…

cross, he prayed… hard… for the repose of the souls of those who had died. And, the souls of those who were going to… die!

Walter Jackson had entered the Parish at Mooselick. But, it had been 'Durango' who had… left! Father Josua Thomas prayed… hard… for… Hell was coming to Augusta Ridge… wearing a matching pair of .44-.40's!

The Exodusters
The Man From Texas

CHAPTER SEVENTEEN

The heavens were shook by a burst of thunder and angel tears soaked the earth, as Stubblefield Smith and 'Jack' Hayes Ward waited to… ambush… the gunman… 'Durango'.

Filling both glasses with 'frontier corn', Mayor Anse Talbert's smiling hoot was, "Hell, ya pay ya taxes, helped with the building of the school house 'n took money outa ya pocket ta help buy medicine for the Crow Tribe. Main thing… ya aint broke no laws… here! Ya past… is ya past. Son, we all got one. So, re-lax. Ya know I'm up fer relection next month… don't ya?"

Tossing back a deep swig of the 'home' brew that was said ta give a man the feelin he dun swallered a lit kerosene lamp, 'Durango' answered, "I shore did… Anse. And I want ta contribute a hundred dollars." In public, the pair referred to each other as… Mayor… and Mister. 'Durango' knew Anse from their 'border-river days'. Anse had worked as a gambler, who sometimes dealt from the bottom of the… deck.

"It be a big help ta me if ya kept ya… 'killin'… out in the county. Times is changin. Most folks don't cotton ta 'killin' in town. Not like ya know, the old days," the Mayor said as he filled both glasses… again.

"Due ma best… Anse. Might not be my call ta make. Due ma best." 'Durango' gulped the firewater, touched the lid of his hat, and left.

Riding out of Augusta Ridge 'Durango' knew it 'payed' to have friends in high places. Especially, friends who us ta deal from the bottom of the… deck!

Nearing Morton's Forks, 'Durango' glanced skyward and noticed that God's window to the earth had been scrubbed near clean of clouds.

His survival instinct caught sight of near two… naw… closer ta three hundred yards to his right the 'Stellar' beauty of a grove. A grove that was absent of… any… wild game activity. The flash came first. Next the zinging of the heavy caliber slugs, from Henry repeating rifles. The slugs cut the overhanging brush. And… almost… 'Durango's'… life!

The man from Texas dismounted. Secured his horse and… watched. And… waited. Some might have wondered… who? 'Durango' wanted to know… why? That eerie feeling and the tenseness in his belly told him 'they be the 'ones'… killed… Matthew! But… how… could he get to them?

One thing was sure. They, whoever the hell they were, couldn't get out. Not unless they… died! And he couldn't get in. Not unless he… died!

'Durango' could do nothing. Not until… dark.

"Damn, almost had him," yelled 'Jack' Hayes Ward. "Almost… aint… accountin," was Stubblefield Smith's retort.

Ward continued, "Caint get ta him now. Caint get paid till he be dead. To near dark. We be a collectin our pay at sunrise…

It was dark. The position of the moon indicated it was 2 or 3 a.m.

He had changed into the dark shirt, one of the two extras, in his saddle bags.

He covered his hands and face… with… mud.

He slept… soundly.

He had not moved for near an hour. It was close ta dawn.

He learned forward, shifted his long gun and dozed.

He slept… soundly.

He sat up… straight. Felt a tingling sensation and then… great pain… as the knife plunged, to the hilt, into his… back. He was halfway ta 'hell' as the blade sliced across his throat… the… smell… of the dead killer's loosed bowels was so… strong… it should have alerted the sleeping Stubblefield Smith.

It did not. Smith continued to… sleep!

Death was… smiling… as he waited in the shadows.

He was… almost… awake.

As sleep stampeded from his eyes, his head began to clear just in time to be faced with two figures, both of them 'Durango' and both of them wielding… death!

His head… cleared…

As death kissed him 'full' on the lips.

CHAPTER EIGHTEEN

Killin musta made O'l Sol mad! It were… shore… hot! The ride back inta town was slowed by the two dead gunmen, face down on their mounts, following behind him.

He still had no answer as ta… why? But he 'knew' they be the ones who had… killed… Matthew. He remembered 'Jack' and 'Jack' worked for! He knew there would be others but… why? Why? was not what Sever Bound were ponderin, but… who? As the second fusillade hit around him. Sever had begun to walk up a new born calf, outa a marshy spot, when the first shots rung out. 'Bo' had scampered. Takin with him Sever's long gun, ammunition, and… water! Sever were… shore… thirsty. He had 'five beans in his wheel'… his cartridge belt was near full. He were… shore… thirsty!

As luck would have it, the mortuary was at the opposite end of town. Nothin like ridin through 'Main Street', in broad daylight, with two dead bodies acomin up behind ya. Townies, visitors and friends got a good-lookie-see. A damn good-lookie-see.

Terry Sun wasn't sure of his target. If only his target would cooperate.. a bit. Terry Sun would be sure!

Sever was cussin… hisself… fer getting caught in a near cross-fire siteachion. The black man behind him did not worry him, as much as the 'ya-hoo' in fronta him. The 'ya-hoo' appeared to be a better… shot! The slug from his Henry Repeatin rifle caught

Sever just above his gunbelt, knocking him to his knees. That was the bad, the good was, when Sever fell, Terry Sun rose up fer a lookie-see. What the black assassin saw as a .45 L.C. greetin' from the downed outlaw/rancher. The bullet hit Sun above his top lip, tore upward into his cranial cavity, and exited through the left side of his head. The force were such, it ripped away the paid killer's ear and upper cheek.

As eternity enveloped him, Terry Sun 'admitted' he had always been a better rustler, then he were… a… gunhand.

'Durango' had just finished layin out 'Jack' Hayes Ward and Stubblefield Smith with the help of Bowers McGee at the mortuary.

The mortuary which was… McGee's stablery.

Bowers McGee was Augusta Ridge's Mortician. He ran a fair stablery. When he were not preparing the 'dearly departed' fer their… last… ride!

"I'll be wantin ta sell the hosses, tack 'n guns for a smart price. Whatcha be offerin?," asked… the man from Texas.

"Be willin ta pay… hum… lets say… three hunert fer the whole kit 'n caboodle," was the stable owner's reply.

Glancing at the two 'dearly depart'… 'Durango' said, "Four hunert 'n itsa deal."

"Agreed," with the response.

Turning ta leave, 'Durango' was confronted by the manager of the stablery, Frank Viking, who huffed past. From the time Walter had rid inta Augusta Ridge, Viking had not taken to him. Walter, did not know… why?

Headed up Main Street, 'Durango' ran abreast a grim faced Hope Dungraver.

One down and… the Henry Rifle's burst interrupted the wounded Sever Bound as he tried to figure a way of getting a 'clear' shot at his 'opponent'.

From his vantage point in the dry underbrush, the tobacco chewin Booker Bert let fly with a long… brown… stream.

Bert could only glean blips of his wounded… prey! He was in no hurry ta get what Terry had… catched. Damn… what a way to die!

"Sheriff, with all due respect, you have become like a bad case-'o-crabs caught in a low class whorehouse. You keep turning up… everywhere."

"Who were the two dead men… Walter?," Dungraver asked. Apparently overlookin the insult.

"One was a fella named 'Jack' Hayes Ward. Didn't know the other… unfortunate," 'Durango' answered.

"Poster Boys?," was the lawman's query.

"Don't know… Sheriff. I do know whatever they was, agin me, they was long on dreams 'n short on… skill!"

"Know… this… 'Durango', you have not violated any law, yet, in Montana Territory, be sure you… don't!"

Adjustin his hat, the outlaw, turned rancher, spoke, "It shore would be something, me 'n you a swappin… lead. Yessir, it shore would be something!"

Walter noticed this was the <u>first</u> time the lawman had addressed him as 'Durango'.

He… shore… were thirsty. The 'seepin' wound in his side were not helping his sit'cheation'. He didn't have his horse. He didn't have his Winchester. He didn't have extra ammunition. He didn't… he did have the 'makins'… and… <u>matches</u>!."

Sippin the cool liquid from his canteen, Booker Bert wondered how long it would take the 'shot' man ta die. Seeins as how his target were without the necessaries, water, bullets, 'n something ta ride outa his pre-dicament.

'Durango' could feel the Sheriff's steely gaze as he walked toward the Steak "N Taters. Working ta stay alive had made him <u>hungry</u>.

The wind was low but, it was blowing in the right direction. Using the dense foliage for cover, he crawled to the edge of the dry underbrush.

The paid killer had 'spected a lots o' thangs but, not… fire! The smoke had begun ta get heavy. His mount was in a thicket out fifty foot from him. He was 'bankin' he could run faster 'n a dyin man could… shoot!"

Booker Bert 'banked'… wrong. Sever's bullet hit him square between the shoulder blades. Booker Bert fell… dead… as his horses' reins slipped through his fingers.

Sever Bound raised up enough to watch his 'unknown' assailant die… and… ta catch the deflected impact of a .50 Cal. sharps slug.

The blow from the awesomely pervading weapon cascaded the wounded outlaw/rancher deep into the marshy ravine, out of harms way(?).

Grant Minor had seed enough men… die. He 'knowed' Sever Bound had gone under. Terry Sun was dead. Booker Bert was dead. Hell, they was all dead!

Placing his Sharps in the rifle boot, Grant stepped into the saddle and sauntered leisurely towards Augusta Ridge… and a… drink!

The Exodusters
The Man From Texas

CHAPTER NINETEEN

It had come a hard freeze that night. Some would say, later, it were what saved… his… life!

Sever Bound had been discovered during a morning hunt by Crow warriors Many Ravens and Standing Buffaloe. The had taken him to the lodge of sub chief 'Comes-the-Horse'.

The Shaman and Dr. Harter Lords, from over at Mooselick, had done what they could. It was now a matter of wait and see. It was now in God's hands!

He were in bad… condition. It hurt just ta think. But think is what he had to do. Who was they? Why had they been so 'hell' bent on killin… him? As he fought passing into unconciousness he 'knew' he must warn… Walter!

While tightening his cinch, he seed the Crow brave approachin, rifle at the ready. The conversation with Junellen… the gunfight… the Sheriff… the letter from Grea… and now… this!

Where was Sever? It had been near four day.

The Crow spoke in sign. Said his name were Standin Buffaloe. Said, 'He Who Always Wore A Gun' was <u>needed</u> at the Crow village. Heading out Walter thought, so far so good, he hadn't been shot at… yet.

"Kilt two of o'um, more'n likely still whar they fell. Never seed nary um afore." The short conversation had left the minding Sever exhausted. Doc. Lords, who was standing next to Walter, had just informed his healing and lucky patient he would walk with a limp… for some time!” Sever was lucky Doc Lords last patient had… died.

“I wouldn’t try to move him no time soon. It maybe another week or more before he can be taken back to the ranch. Had that Sharps slug come full force, Mr. Bound would be walking and talking with Jesus! Need anything or he takes a bad turn, best send for me immediately Mr. Jackson. With those words, the medico turned and departed.

Walter waited until he could no longer hear Harter Lords buggy before he spoke. “I know who the bastards bee. Don’t… know why… yet! Where be it did the killin take place?”

“Down in the “South section, marshy portion. I’m sorry partner. Can’t seems ta…” The laudanum was working, Sever had fallen into a deep sleep in mid-sentence.

Walter saw to his friend’s comfort and, then eased away slowly, to find the ones dun the shootin. ‘Durango’ was going to see to it they fell into a deep sleep. One from which they would never… awake!

Walter had no difficulty locating the sight of the shooting. It had happencd on the [illegible] Ranch. He found what was left of the two murderers for hire. The one out near the small clump of trees was swollen so far beyond recognition, his own ma woulda had trouble i’dentifyin him. The other one, the animals had got ta him. What had not been ate, did not match the ‘mortal’ remains of a human being.

‘Durango’ buried what was left of the two men, placed markers and, made the sign of the… cross. It took near two hours to complete the ‘grim’ task. It did not take two hours ta pick up the trail fo the man who had use the Sharps rifle. 'Durango' followed the assassin's tracks straight inta Augusta Ridge.

"Frank be shore ta lock the shed. S'pears ta be more new folk' round den usual. don't won't nothing growin feets 'n walkin away"... "Yessuh, Mista Bowers. I shorely will," was Frank Viking's reply, as he stumbled backward into the darkened room. Lighting the lamp, Frank received such a shock, he was glad he had emptied his bowels after that 'hearty' noonday meal at the Steak "N Taters, or he might have done so at this moment!

Standing in the shadows was a big black man, with two big black guns aimed in Frank's direction.

"Listen... Mista, I gots maybe three, four dollas, dat all. Ya be welcome ta it, jes don't shoot... pu-leeze!" Frank always said 'please' and 'thank you' when it mattered most. It sure as hell mattered now!

"Easy Frankie, easy. I'm a barer o' glad tidins. Dis har is a chance ta fatten ya pockets 'n rid ya self o' ya chief rival fer Ms. Junellen, or... die! Ya intrasted?"

Walter entered the Steak 'N Taters by the side door, took a table in the corner with his back to the wall. He ordered a beer, took a few deep pulls, 'n looked fer the one shot his friend.

It were short order ta spottin the 'brazen' bastard. He sat near the up front window. The 'deadly' Sharps leaned against the wall. When the cook's daughter entered from the kitchen, carryin a coupla plates o' grub, 'Durango' quietly called, "Marria... por favor..."

It is amazing how attentive to detail a professional man can be toward somethings, but so blind ta other things.

For 'Durango' it was not coming to the realization that his speed and skill with the instruments of death strapped to his side were both a… blessing… and a… curse!

Once a 'gunman', aways a…

For Grant Minor it was never once looking toward the rear of the Steak 'N Taters. His relaxed, alcohol-aided, state led him to pay for his meal, tip his hat to the waitress and ride off to… die! 'Durango' observing from the kitchen's partially opened door, saw Grant Minor ride in the direction of Will Parks Creek.

Checkin his back trail, Grant watching from cover, saw the Crow brave and his Squaw travlin at a safe distance behind him. The brave musta been… sick. He had a blanket pulled up 'round him'. Grant hoped it were not Cholera. It be deadly 'n catchin. W.W. rode across Will Parks Creek, Grant kept his eye on the Indians fordin downstream, at a safe distance and disappearing into the woods.

"Half-way… thar, Sever bees dead." Lighting a cigar, Grant looked at his… friend… and Cohort, smiling Minor said, "What say ya W.W.?"

"Whar be Terry Sun 'n Booker?'

"Dead… boss, dead!," was the reply.

Without apparent remorse, Walker said, "Price a man pays sometimes in a dan-jes occapasion." Equally emotionless, “What... we gonna due?,” asked his second-in-command.

“Well... dun find us a extra hand. A ‘Lovelorn’ want ta ‘liminate’ his competshion, sad as ‘hell’ reason ta wants ta kill a man. But, it aint ma reasonin. I throwed in a few dollas ta up the... ante.” Dismounting to adjust his riggin, Walker added, “Gonna stop over inta town till dark, then I bees drifin towards the J Ranch. Settle up wid ‘Durango’! If’n he aint thar, you ‘n me be meetin ‘round noon at the Smitty’s. We be tryin at him... again!”

“Shore... nuf, dun ate ta much. Gonna finish ma smoke ‘n then a siesta. Bees finding som whars nar the livery ta bed down fer the night,” Grant said rubbing his supper filled belly.

Walker looked on as his... friend... scrunched into the side of a nearby tree. Grant sat facing the creek, re-lit his cigar and got plumb... comfortable.

Stepping into the saddle, Walker felt duty-bound to remind his... friend... of who and what they had ‘conspired’ ta... kill.

“Amigo, dontcha go agettin too re-laxed. Walter Jackson be a fella who are amite bettern his repatachion. Look ta ya self!”

“W.W., if’n I don’t be aknowin better, I were be thankin ya were ma Maw. Cant be true. Seeins as how she were a diff-farant color ‘n twice as purdy,” Grant shouted with a roar.

“My friend, that there were a rip-snortin, thigh-slapper. Hope I do nots ail ma self laughin,” came Walker’s reply, as he rode toward Augusta Ridge.

He awoke or, thought he was awake, with a… start. He focused. He saw pure beauty! Less than twenty foot from him, in the middle of the creek, sat that Injun squaw on her painted pony. But, this time she were wearin… nuthin. Not a damn thread! Jes sittin there. Grant hadn't been with woman… how long were it? He took a quick lookie-see. To his left. Well, by damn him, he were gonna be wid one… today!

Droppin his Sharps, he strode at her. As the heat in his loins rose, he 'swore' he caught a whiff of her… womanhood!

What he caught was the cat-quick movement of 'Durango', who had been crouched underwater behind some rocks.

Minor had a second ta grab fer his belly gun. He needed more time that that. The one-time outlaw's first slug hit the paid assassin smack in the chest. Stumbling forward, Grant clutched for his hand gun, with his hope fading and his mind reeling, he 'cursed' himself for not having his… Sharps!

'Durango's' second shot hit just below the dry glucher's nose. Exiting at the base of his skull and severed his spine. Screaming, Grant Minor vaulted into Will Parks Creek. He made not another… sound! Pushing himself through the water, 'Durango' moved close to the floating dead man. He then fired a 'makesure' that obliterated the agony-filled face of the hired… killer.

The finality of death proved as "unkind" as… 'Durango's'… bullets.

Floating behind the… floatin… "quiet" gunman were his… 'leavins', of all he had dun ate, of all he were ‘airy gonna… ate. Damn Grim Reapa… ‘spected nary man, woman, ‘er… chile!

In the Dime Store Western Novels, some writers made killing seem ta be ‘romantic’, reality o’ the thang be, killing were an ‘ugly business’…

The Exodusters
The Man From Texas

CHAPTER TWENTY

PART ONE

The Rev. Horticie Merced 'cracked' the whip to rush the buggy horse along. He didn't understand 'the rush' to get to Augustu Ridge. By his count, fifteen more miles and they would be there! The trip had been… overbearing. Troublesome weather. Terrible roads. If he had not agreed, his daughter would have faced the difficulties and dangers of the weather and travel… alone! That was unthinkable. Besides the Church, Grea was all he had!

"Daughter is there trouble?"

"Yes, father. Sever Bound has been badly wounded. Walter is looking for the people who injured his friend."

The Reverend recognized it would accomplish, nothing, to recite his disagreement with, and about, Grea's relationship with the outlaw who had become a rancher.

He 'knew' 'Durango' would always be… a… gunman! "Grea, I pray Walter will be safe. I know how important he is to you. Daughter, I want you to be… happy!"

"Thank you father," was his daughter's response. The remainder of the trip was spent in… silence!

The Reverend, often, wondered if living in Montana's capitol city, Horsehead's Creek, was far enough away from 'Durango' and the killings which seemed to follow him. And, his matching .44-40's.

Rev. Merced did not want his only child hurt. Emotionally or otherwise!

Grea stared to her right. She knew about... Junellen. She would never allow time, tide, distance, killings, or... Junellen Kaye... to come between her and Walter.

She wondered if Walter 'touched' Junellen the way he 'touched' her. Grea immediately wiped that image from her mind.

She thought about the first time the man from Texas had... it had been her... first... time! Grea smiled, inwardly, at how 'wet and squashy' her organ for copulation had become. Just like the rain soaked, muddy, road.

Grea... 'knew'... without... him, her heart would... hurt. as it had before he... smiled... his way into her life.

... Some... women needed a man for all the... wrong... reasons!

... Some... women needed a man for all the... right... reasons...

... She... needed... Walter. Right or wrong!

Nick Jones

PART TWO

"I, always… always liked ya. But ya don't's seems ta be alikin me that… aways. Der gonna be troubles comin ta town. Bad troubles."

"Frank I like you. You are a considerate man. I regret I cannot feel toward you, the way you feel toward me. Frank, please, what trouble are you talking about?"

"Dat der… nigga. Ya naw, dat Walter. Ms. Junellen, he aint naw good fer nobody. Nobody. 'Specially a… lady like ya. Nigga aint nutin but a gunhan 'n he awanted everwahars."

"Frank! That simply is not true! He is only wanted in Arizona territory. And, there are questions regarding his guilt."

"He shore nuf dun it. I knows he dun it," Frank Viking exclaimed empathically!

"As I said Frank," Junellen continued, "There are questions regarding his guilt! There were no witnesses. Folks just believe he is guilty. Some just 'want' him to be guilty. He has not committed any crimes while he had been in… Montana territory… Frank!"

"Nun dat a man kin proves. He bees guilty! Does ya knows 'bout dat preaching man's daughter he bess wid?"

"Frank," Junellen shouted as she thought 'yes… I know all about Ms. Grea Merced', "That has nothing to do with Walter's 'supposed' guilt in the 'supposed' Arizona Bank robbery."

"Does ya knows she were in town, dis very minute?"

"No. I did not," was Junellen's 'tart' reply. She had become quite agitated with the livery foreman for directing so personal and so intimate an attack!

"I da one put up da buggy, 'n hoss fer her 'n her daddy. Jes bees shore ta stay away from town tamarra 'round noon."

On that ominous note, Frank Viking said good-bye, mounted his horse and rode in the direction of…the  ranch.

Why in that… direction?

Junellen watched the man, who so disliked the man she loved, ride into the evening shadows.

With her heart racing, she was confronted with <u>two</u> immediate tasks! Warn… Walter. Get to Augusta Ridge before… noon.

… and the bards say, "hell hath no fury like a <u>woman</u> scorned!"

The Exodusters
The Man From Texas

PART THREE

For those who had prayed for a bright, sunny and warm Sunday morning… God had delivered! It was fitting for today. The Sabbath! This day of beauty in Augusta Ridge, Montana. This day of new beginnings for some. This day of… death… for others!

He was tired. A long night of watching them, watch him, contributed to his fatigue. Well, they thought they… watched… him. Actually, behind the pulled shade, it had been the new cook. Undressing and preparing for bed in 'his room'.

He had been far way watching with binoculars. W.W. had arrived just as the sun was saying goodnight to the sky. Frank Viking came a short time later.

The hummingbirds had begun their morning serenade when he eased from his position on the hill overlooking the J-Ranch. Checking his vest watch, it were near 6 a.m. He led his horse for a distance. Mounted and rode like hell for Augusta Ridge. His grandparents had taught him it were not nice ta keep company waitin.

'Durango' would be ready when W.W. Walker and Frank Viking got ta town.

"What's he doin down der?", probed the livery foreman. "Jes left the 'little house' outback. From whar we at, did not see nutin but the top o' his hat", was the response. "We gots… long… guns. Shoulda started da dance", Viking spat as he watched the side entrance, near the corral. "sho' nuf… Frankie. Wid does (those) hans (hands) out front, we never be spending ourn pay. I knows ya were new ta dis har but, if'n a man gets casual like, he gets… dead! 'Member, never rush a… killin. Ole W.W. be a tryin ta school ya!"

Eric Lyle did not know why his new employer had insisted he meet him at… Ms. Junellen's. She had brought the message. Eric was told to bring a horse, some range clothes and, a… hat. Was the request odd? Or was the request odd because it were near midnight before the task were completed? And, Lyle was in his boss' bedroom, preparing for… bed?

Following his instructions to the letter, Eric dressed Mr. Jackson's shirt and wearing one of his matching .44's, headed out to saddle Mr. Jackson's favorite… horse! Above all else, he was to keep his back facin the lush open eastern range, which served as a 'welcome mat' for those entering the J- Ranch. Eric Lyle, as Walter Jackson, rode west with range foreman, Micah Nelson, ranch hands Pete Antrose and Chuck Gerald. They rode toward the hill country.

"'Pars everybody gon. We can sneak down fer a look see."

"Damn Frank. Dontcha knows der be a gun somewhars lined on dat front doe (door)," stated Walker. "Boy… if'n ya gon work wid me, ya gotta learns dis har… trade! Maybees I dun paid ya too much 'er I bee 'spectin too much from ya."

Viking's angry retort, "I jes wants ta kill dat… nigga. Dead, dead, dead!"

"Frank, Ole W.W. bee moe (more) den happy wid jes… one… dead. Dontcha bee letting ya heart cause ya ta lose ya… head!"

Walker and his duely 'admonished pupil' left their cover and roof for Augusta Ridge. To wait... ta kill... the man from Texas!

Maria brought the pot of coffee to the pretty woman, the woman who loved the man Maria had watched... kill... a hired killer. The killer named Grant Minor.

'Durango' had paid her will for her services. She knew him from his border-river days. He had been kind to her for no apparent reason, which resulted in no immediate 'profit'.

At the creek he could have had her, if he had chose. Instead, he was a gentleman. 'Durango' turned his back as she rode to retrieve her clothes. Her open 'cash register' had netted... No Sale!

Maria passed in front of the Steak 'N Taters bay window in time to see the attractive Junellen Kay enter Sheriff Hope Dungraver's office. "Morning, Ms. Junellen, shore be a fine Sunday. Now aint it?"

"Good morning Sheriff. It is a beautiful God given day. I am afraid it will be disrupted with... gunfire!"

Wiping his mouth with the table napkin, Rev. Merced cleard his throat and said, "It is most gracious that I have been 'asked' to speak to a combined congreation of both coloreds and whites, don't you think?"

"Yes, yes it is very nice, father," was the Reverand's daughter's response. Her mind was elsewhere. It was across the street in Sheriff Dungraver's office with... Junellen Kaye.

On the third knock, the maid answered the door. "Good morning Sheriff. How you bee?"

"I bee fine Daisy, 'cuse me... goodmorning ta ya. I must see Mayor Talbert right away!" This way Sir', the maid said leading a 'harried' looking Dungraver into the dinning area where Anse Talbert was finishing his breakfast.

The Mayor was normally not up at so 'ungodly' an hour, but... it were election time. Here he was up, dressed, sober(?) and had left his 'favorite whore' asleep in his... bed! The thangs a man <u>must</u> do ta get relected!

"Sit down Hope. Daisy bring the Sheriff a cup o' coffee. You will be joining us for the combined religious service wontcha. H.D.?"

"Yessuh, I plan on bein at the religious festivities. but listen ta this, hell is a comin ta town in the form o' Walter Jackson. Ifn he aint here aready."

"Walter been real good 'about folloin the law. Said if he were ta be in a shootin scrape, he'd be tryin ta keep it in da county. What dun happened ta bring Walter ta town wid blood in his eye?" Melody Hart waved at her niece as she drove her flat-bed wagon toward Rounded Rock Bible Church. Melody would be singing in the mixed choir and wanted to get to town a little early. As the Widow Hart stepped from the wagon, she saw her niece, Junellen, step into an... alleyway.

Walter Jackson as an outlaw, as a gunman had survived when others perished! He had succeeded when others failed!

He was... the best!

He was the... best... because he 'knew' the speed of a man's gun was no match for the speed of a man's... mind!

Walter Jackson was... the... best!

He knew, he waited. He had a plan to kill those who were comin ta... kill... him!

"Junellen... darling, I need your help. Men are comin ta town ta try 'n kill me. Frank is one of 'um"

"Walter, I knew Frank may have been... jealous(?) But... murder?"

"Yeah... murder! Take ya hoss down ta the livery 'n..."

"Yest sweetheart. Walter, I will do... anything... I'll..."

"Yes mamam, I 'believe' you will. Time is short. I'll be needin..."

"You need... what?"

AS a 'desperate' Frank Viking, and his equally emotional opposite untithered their horses, Frank spat out, "What... now!"

"Tis a Sunday 'n a beautiful one at dat. Beins as how I'm a man o' culture 'n breedin..."

With exasperation Frank howled, "Ya gonna go ta da church house?"

"Naw... Frankie. I'm gonna go'n get me a drank!"

Round Rock Bible Church didn't get its name from any, nearby, that is distinguishing land marks. The church's inauspicious beginning, began the day the 'somewhat' disheveled Reverand Tory Bend ambled into town... on foot.

Seeins as how the most Reverand Bend was on the south end of a dollar going north, the Reverand had no place to lay his head. Or anything else he was carrying. But, Tory Bend was an honest man. And, like the priest over at Mooselick, a God 'sent' man.

Thus, the Spirit lead him to a most… beautiful… spot. About a mile or so outside of Augusta Ridge. On the very… spot… where he had laid his head, some thirty years ago, the church's foundation had been built!

Now here he stood. Overlooking a congreagtation mixed in both color and denomination, he prepared himself to speak.

The Reverand Bend observed a full pulpit, a full choir stand, and a full church. For those who were 'aware' of what was about to happen, in Augusta Ridge, and Reverand Bend was aware. They 'knew' the only parties missing were the man from Texas. And, the men he intended… ta… kill!

Rev. Bend sincerely desired to conquer the nervous habit of adjusting his tie before he spoke, "My Christian friends there are many examples in the Holy Bible which teach us that a people divided, undecided, and unwilling to come to an understanding among themselves will not… survive!"

"Look down yonda nar da livery. It bee Junellen's hoss. I'm gonna go 'n see ifn she bee dar."

"Careful… Frankie. I'm gonna get off here. The saloon. Take my hoss wid ya."

"Alrite. I bee back. I bee back!"

"Shore Frankie… shore"

Frank slowly eased open the door to the stable. In the dusky shadows he saw… nothing. He bolted into the nearest stall… nothing, he carefully began to raise his head… something! The slug struck close to his left cheek. Frank dove back into the stall's muck, grateful, he hadn't lost his… head!

"Dat ya… Walter?"

"Its… me, Frank. Its me. Come on out 'n lets talk a bit."

Frank fired two rapid shots in the direction of where he 'thought' Walter was. Follow by, "I aint a talkin ta ya. Ya murderin black bastard."

'Durango' threw a diversionary object to his far right. Became motionless and… waited!

"I aint a fallin fer dat old trick, nigga. Gots ta do better 'n dat", Viking shouted.

"Alright… Frank. Here's a present fer ya. I jes left Junellen 'n she was awarin these! Before I took 'um off her."

No response!

Tossing the 'item' within reach of the hidden liveryman, 'Durango' said, "Why don't ya pick 'um up 'n rub 'um under ya nose? May as well. Her 'scents' as close as ya'll ever be gittin ta her… 'precious pot'."

Frank saw the 'item'. The bloomers with the initials J.K. on the legs. The bloomers with the slight discoloration in the… crotch.

A response!

Frank went… wild!

In Frank's haste. In Frank's anger. Frank heard, almost, nothing. He heard the third click of his hammer on another spent cartridge. Frank did hear… that!

Frantically trying to reload his weapon, Frank heard what those in the 'brotherhood of the gun' affectionately called the 'three clicks of fate'.

One... I'm shore gonna miss this har place.
Two... A prayer. If'n ya believes in such.
and
Three... Welcome ta... hell!

With one .44-.40... empty and, leaving the other in case he were... charged... Walter had eased the black-powder .36 Cal. Navy Colt from its... resting... place.

At close range, what the slugs had dun ta... Frank...

'Durango' reloaded and holstered his Sheriff's Model .36 Cal. Navy Colt. On his way ta say 'adios' ta W.W., 'Durango' dropped Junellen's bloomers over Frank Viking's bloody... puke-stained... face! Walking uptown, he 'knew' there was only two places Ole W.W. should be. The hotel. The saloon. Bees too early fer sleepin! The saloon.

'Durango' pulled up short in front of Augusta Ridge's Saturday night... 'hotspot'.

"Payday... William. I'm waitin." AS he casually reloaded the pearl-handled .44-.40. W. William Walker knew the voice. Just like he had 'known' the man behind the voice would be... coming. The only bartender the 'Dew Drop Inn' had ever knowed said, "Company callin... Mista."

"Yeah. He gonna bee one 'hellava' houseguest," Walker replied. He then drained his glass of the fiery liquid and said, "Shore bees hard ta get 'good' help now-a-days, aint it?"

"Yessuh, shore is. Ya gon have to do it yourself?", was the bartender's question.

"Yessuh," came Walker's answer.

Sauntering through the saloons' batwing doors, W. William Walker stepped into the street to face the man he had been paid ta... kill!

From the position of the sun, it were near two o'clock. Church meetin would soon be endin!

Easing his coat open Walker said, "The man from Texas."

"Yup. The man from Texas. Why...? Why, me?"

"Somebody wont 'cha dead real... bad."

"The old man 'n Sever?"

"Extre larder fer da fattening," said the Paid Assassin.

"But... why?", asked the puzzled gunman turned rancher.

"Adios... Walter."

"Adios... William. And, be damned ta ya!"

It happened in the blink of an eye.

'Durango' fired three shots in rapid succession. The first hit Walker in the upper chest. Standing the 'Killer For Pay'... erect.

The second bullet struck just under the bleeding gunman's right eye. Bringing forth both gushing blood and... gore! The third slug wasn't necessary. 'Durango' fired the shot out of pure cussed 'meaness'.

A 'credit' to his profession, as he was dyin, W. Will Walker did clear leather and, fired a shot. A shot into… nowhere. His loosed bowels and bladder went… everywhere!

"Ya see it?"

"Yeah… yeah. I shore did saw it. Were a fair one," was the bartender's answer.

By the time the church crowd arrived, W. William Walker was resting, in the eternal sleep, next to his 'emotional opposite' down at the livery!

Taking a seat in front of the man from Texas, who sat with his back to one of the 'Dew Drop Inns' walls, Sheriff Dungraver politely asked, "What kinda hand did Walker 'n Frank Viking… play?"

"Aces 'n eights", came the reply.

"Witnesses?"

"A… witness!"

"Alrite. Were a fair one?"

"Ya… bet… it were a… fair… one!", said 'Durango'.

"There bee two ladies awaitin out front… fer… ya."

"Two… two. I was a hopin at least one would bee, but… drinks on me Sheriff." Leaving money on the table, touching the lid of his hat, the outlaw turned rancher exited through the saloon's back door. And, rode rapidly toward the Ranch.

PART FOUR

Racing onto the Slash's 'welcome mat', 'Durango' shouted, "Pete get this rig on 'chock'. Tell the cook ta pack grub fer the trail. Bee shore ta load me heavy wid .44-.40's. 'n make shore I got ma long gun"...

"Yes sir, Mr. Jackson!"

Blasting through the front door, 'Durango' yelled, 'Sever... Server... where ya at?"

"Over here pardner, what's all the ruckus?"

"Whar's ma black hat 'n ma .44?," asked a seemingly frustrated 'Durango'.

"In ya room. Walter... whar bee the fire?," came his friend's response.

Moving hurridly into his room, to gather the items in question, Walter gushed, "I kilt W. William Walker 'n Frank Viking." Holding the ornament up for view, Walter said, "Walker had this har on 'um! He had a wad o' green backs ta boot. I find who this 'doodad' belongs ta 'n... ya seed it's likes afore?"

"Nope. It be Injun jewelry. Only place I aknows of wid them thar stones is... New Mexico territory," was Bound's answer. "Alrite then. Sever har's how we gonna play it..."

As the sky was changing from blue to black they arrived. One from the East. One from the West. Love... has a way, sometimes, of eliminating pleasantries. They blurted, "Where is... Walter?"

"He bee gon Ms. Grea, Ms. Junellen. Left more'n two hour ago," said Sever.

"Where did he go?", was the combined response.

"He made me swar not ta utter a work. Wontchall please, Ms. Junellen, Ms. Grea, come inside fer supper? Itsa getting… late," requested the 'mendin' outlaw turned rancher.

The Exodusters
The Man From Texas

PART FIVE

'Chock' snorted and fought the reign's amite before plunging inta Will Parks Creek. Clearing the far side, 'Durango' was a man in a trance. His heart bore the weight of a conestoga wagon… for good reason. God, he loved Grea. He loved Junellen. Somehow, he 'knew' he would marry… that would come later. What was important, now, were who wanted him… dead! And why?

He turned his mount south, toward New Mexico territory. Along with the creeping shadows invading the disappearing Montana landscape, came that eerie feeling and that tenseness in his belly!

Who?

Why?

ABOUT THE AUTHOR

NICK JONES IS AN HONORABLY DISCHARGED VIETNAM ERA VETERAN FROM SOUTH BEND. INDIANA.

JONES HOLDS UNDERGRADUATE DEGREES IN PSYCHOLOGY AND SOCIOLOGY.AND A GRADUATE DEGREE IN SOCIOLOGY.HE IS PURSUING HIS DOCTORATE IN SOCIOLOGY. JONES SERVES AS AN ADJUNCT FACULTY

MEMBER AT SEVERAL INSTITUTIONS.HIS COMPANY, W.T.J. FILMS, SPECIALIZES IN WESTERN PROJECTS CONCERNING BLACK AMERICAN MEN WHO HELPED BUILD THE AMERICAN WEST! JONES WROTE, PRODUCED, DIRECTED AND STARRED IN THE GROUND BREAKING WESTERN BASS REEVES. U.S~DEPUTY MARSHAL. REEVES, AN EX-SLAVE, WAS AMERICA'S FIRST BLACK U.S. DEPUTY MARSHAL.HIRED IN 1876 BY THE "HANGING" JUDGE.

THE HAT, GUN, AND GUNBELT JONES WORE IN THE PROJECT ARE IN THE COLLECTION OF THE NATIONAL COWBOY HALL OF FAME!

Printed in the United States
1066500003B/412

9 781403 389398

Mya & Markell
A Hood Love Story

By

Meah-Shawn'Tae

Synopsis

Mya Draught is a 24 year old Wellness Nurse born and raised in Los Angeles, Ca. Mya worked hard for everything she has. She was left orphaned at 16 years old by her mother who died of a drug overdose and her father who was killed during a bank robbery.

Markell "Cash" Castanedez is a 24 year old businessman but not in the legal sense. Markell has all of California on lock with the purest dope you could possibly get your hands on. When Markell and Mya meet sparks immediately fly and they become inseparable not knowing someone very close to them is harboring a secret that could possibly destroy their relationship and everything that they've built.

Malcolm "Mac" Castanedez is a 26yr old businessman and Markell's older brother with a few secrets, one of them being a robbery he committed at the tender age of 18 that led to the death of Mya's father.

Is their love strong enough to make it through all of the secrets and lies? Or is the pain too deep to hold on?

Mya

Beep, Beep, Beep!

The sound of my alarm going off annoyed me, and I was pissed that yet again it was ruining a perfectly good sleep. I had half a mind to hit snooze, just to see how that dream I was having ends.

I shook my head laughing at myself because I knew if I hit snooze, there would be no work today or tomorrow because my ass would be fired.

I threw the covers back and jumped out of bed. The first thing I did was turn on my morning playlist, which consisted of India Arie, Goapele and Alicia Keys, with a dash of Jill Scott. Once my music was flowing through my home speakers, I headed to the bathroom to handle my morning hygiene.

I looked myself over in the mirror and admired how perfectly imperfect I was. My parents named me Mya Draught, I stood 5'2, around 150lbs, with sun kissed brown skin that I got compliments of my Colombian mother and black father. My shoulder length hair was naturally curly and suited my round face perfectly. I was a perfect replica of my mother, the only things I got from my father were his chinky eyes and round nose. My breast were a c cup and I had about two handfuls worth of ass, which wasn't anything to brag about these day with all the Nicki

Minaj's and Kim Kardashian's of the world, but shit it was all mine and I was more than happy with it.

As I started the shower and stood under the water, I thought about everything I had been through in my 24 years of life, from my mother dying of a heroin over dose and my father being killed in front of me.

My life wasn't all that bad growing up, we lived in the bottoms, which is in Inglewood if you're not from Cali. My mom, Ana worked as a manager at a local grocery store and my dad, Michael was a mechanic at a shop him and my uncle owned. My mom hid her drug habit pretty well, to the point where no one knew she was getting high, not even my dad and they were practically inseparable. 8 years ago my life drastically changed, when I lost both my mom and dad on the same day.

My dad had just picked me from tennis practice as usual on Thursday evening, and we rushed to the bank, to make his cash deposits from the shop. As we were about to walk in I stopped to tie my shoes, my dad kept going because it was almost closing time and he hated to have that kind of money on him around our neighborhood.

As I stood back up and began walking toward the bank, I heard what sounded like 3 gun shots and I panicked, I pulled the door open and I saw my dad lying there bleeding from his stomach and mouth. I screamed, as I looked into the eyes of the man who had just possibly killed the only man I loved, and who had been there for me.

The shooter ran passed me, as I fell down and laid my head on my father's chest begging him not to leave me. A couple hours later my uncle on my dad's side had finally taken me home, and as we walked inside we saw my mother's body on the couch with foam and vomit coming from her mouth, and a needle in her arm.

Shaking the thoughts from my mind, I was proud of everything I had accomplished. I was a nurse at a senior living facility in Beverly Hills making great money, and decent hours. My days basically just consisted of passing meds, counting medications and some charting here and there. I loved my job, the only issues were the bitches I worked with, all they did was gossip and if you weren't down to gossip with them, then you better believe your ass was number one on the list of things they would talk about.

Hopping out of the shower I grabbed some scrubs to throw on and headed toward Starbucks for my usual, a vanilla bean frappuccino and a slice of lemon cake. About 20 minutes later I was pulling up to the facility where I worked, and immediately grew annoyed because a new move-in was blocking half of the garage entrance.

Just as I was about to call the receptionist a tall, dark and handsome man came walking out the building and up to my car.

"Sorry Ms. Lady, I was just about to move this truck but I can't figure out how to get around back." I admired him as he spoke, his perfect smile, white teeth and the way his tongue gracefully moved between his lips after he spoke. "Excuse me Ms. Lady did you hear me?" He said, with a chuckle and smirk that had my ass so damn embarrassed.

I cleared my throat and spoke, "No, I mean yes, you can follow behind me. I have the key card to get around back, and I just need you to back up a little bit for me to get through." He nodded and got in his truck, doing just what I asked of him before following me inside.

Markell

As I followed little momma into the garage, I couldn't help but think to myself how good she looked, I licked my lips with the anticipation of getting a view of her when she stepped out of the car. I thought about it for a hot second, then shook the thoughts from my head as we parked.

I was getting out the truck when she approached me, "Did the receptionist give you the elevator code, or explain to you how it worked?" I guess the look on my face gave her the answer because she continued, "Okay, well follow me and I'll show you how to key the code in so you can bring up your stuff. Also I'm going to need your ID before I give you the code and once your finished you can come to my office or have the front desk page me, and I'll bring it to you."

I gave her what she needed, she explained to me how the elevator worked and that shit was complicated as fuck, I would have been standing here looking stupid for hours.

"Thanks Ms., Damn I don't even know your name ma." I rubbed my hand down my face because I was slipping today.

"Draught, Mya Draught." She smiled as she said and shook my hand; damn she was beautiful. I nodded and we went our separate ways.

***

Three and half hours later, my brother Malcolm and I had everything in our mom's room and put together. "Now we just have to get her ass here." My brother said jokingly. I laughed with my brother because he was right.

My mom was just diagnosed with Dementia a few months ago, and even though it was at the beginning stages her worrisome ass neighbors had begun to call my brother and I. Saying my mom was walking around at night, and saying that they were worried about her safety, so we had no choice but to move her into a memory care facility. The problem was my mom has lived in the same house for 20 years, and we just knew getting her to move wouldn't go well.

My mom was a strong woman, she raised my brother Malcolm and I alone after my father bailed out on us around my 10th birthday. We grew up in Inglewood, in a nice 2 bedroom house off of Van Ness and 111th. I watched my mom break her back to take care of us, so I worked my ass off in school so I could get a good job making good money to help out my mom's.

My brother couldn't stand watching her work her ass off, so he linked up with group of niggas that sold light work, such as weed and pills to keep a steady income flowing in. Me being my brother's keeper I couldn't let him be out there by himself, so I linked up with him and we were tripling what he was already making.

My brother wanted to move up in the drug game, so he came up with a plan that he said he didn't want me to know about, just in case it backfired. I wasn't with that shit, but he wasn't budging, so I prayed no matter what my brother made it home and he did.

One night my brother came home with a bag of money, we spent hours counting that shit, which came up to 275 thousand dollars, more than enough for what he had planned. My brother never told me what he did to get that money, and truthfully I never asked, but I had his back no matter what if it ever came back to bite him in the ass, best believe I would right there with him.

I was still pushing myself in school and got a scholarship to UCLA, so I went and took up business. It made my mom's proud, and I knew that with what we had planned my degree would come in handy.

Thanks to all the hard work my brother and I put in, the life I lived now was fucking incredible. We had the entire coast of California on lock with the purest coke you could get your hands on. Our shit came straight from Columbia, from a fat ass Colombian name Ruiz Escobar, our shit ran smoothly. The only thing I was missing in my life was a beautiful woman by my side, to share my life and wealth with, some bad ass kids to spoil and chill with.

I was interrupted from my thoughts by a knock on the door, I opened it and there stood Ms. Draught, soon to be Mrs. Castanendez. "Sorry to interrupt, but I just wanted to see if you'd brought the list of medications your mom is currently taking, as well as her primary care information for her file?"

"I have the complete list, and my assistant should have faxed it over about 30 minutes ago." I couldn't help but notice the smile she kept on her face. Damn she was beautiful. "Okay, great I'll go check the fax machine and get back with you to let you know if we received it, as well as to bring back your ID." Before she could walk away my brother Malcolm grabbed her arm, "Where you running off to beautiful?" She turned around with a mean ass mug on her face before responding to him.

"Get your fucking hands off of me, or you won't have a fucking hand to grab anyone else." She walked up close on him as she spoke, and the fire in her eyes let me know that she was capable of fucking some shit up. My brother through his hands up in mock surrender, and stared at her as if he knew her.

"Calm down lioness, this is my brother Malcolm and he didn't mean any disrespect he cool peoples, you'll see once you get to know him." As I spoke to her, the look on her face was still twisted up and right when I was about to speak again an older white lady came over, "Mya, is everything okay here?" She looked like she didn't know how we could afford such a fine establishment and didn't want us there, but whatever my money was green like everyone else's.

"Yes Kim, everything is fine. I was just explaining to these gentlemen everything I would need to get started on their mother's chart." She gave the lady a warm smile and she walked away. "Markell, when you're finished you can come to my office for your ID, or have the receptionist call me on your way out." With that she walked away, but not before mugging the fuck out of my brother.

"Damn Malcolm, can you not piss off momma's nurses before she even move her ass up in here, please?" I was aggravated with him, he's the oldest yet was always showing his ass. "My bad bro, but damn she had a fat ass and she look like she can take the dick with no problems." I don't know why, but him speaking on her sexually pissed me off and as I closed the door I hemmed his ass up. "Don't ever in your fucking like speak to her, or about her like that again, you hear me?" The look on his face was one of death, but I didn't give a fuck I made my point and he better take heed to that shit brother or not, little mama would be the reason he got fucked up.

"Damn bro my bad, I didn't know you was feeling shorty like that, but you got it I won't fuck with shorty no more, unless she ask me to." He laughed at the last part and I just had to shake my head, because his ass just didn't know when to quit.

Me and brother dapped each other up, and went our separate ways as I got to the receptionist desk to have them call Mya; she informed me that she had my ID and Mya had been called into a meeting. I was disappointed, but work is work so I understood.

As I pulled up to my condo out in Westwood I just felt blessed, not only was I that nigga out here in these Cali streets, but I owned my own company helping young niggas get out the hood with this rapping shit. I had nice cars, a nice ass place to lay my head and a nigga wasn't starving. The only thing I was lacking was a woman to come home to, shit the only woman I was fucking right now was my house keeper, and that bitch was becoming crazy and cling as fuck. She emptied out a whole side of my dresser and started putting shit in there, like who the fuck does that? Just thinking about it had me 38 hot.

Finally making it to my room I grabbed some boxers from my dresser, and headed to take a shower to relax because a nigga had a long ass night ahead of him.

Mya

I was sitting at my desk putting together charts for out new residents when I looked up and noticed Markell's sexy ass. Damn! That man was fine. He looked just like Kofi Siriboe, from that show Queen Sugar. He was tall and handsome with rich dark skin, His eyes were dark as if they held many secrets, secrets that he was dying to share and I wouldn't mind being the person that he opened up to.

Before he spotted me checking him out, I put my head down and got back to work. I was relieved that today was Friday, which meant me and my best friend Naya, would be hitting up club Carbon in Culver City tonight around 9. While on break I began to mentally put together my outfit in my head, so I didn't spend a lot of time doing it when I got home.

When I was clocking back in I heard yelling coming from a residents room down the hall, "Hell no Markell, take me the fuck home now! I will not allow you to lock me up like I'm crazy, I am not crazy!" His mother yelled while hitting him in the chest right before she broke down crying, he looked lost he didn't know what to do. He tried reasoning with her, but he was going about it all wrong.

The yelling continued, so I went toward them to try and speak with his mother. "Good morning Mr. Castanendez, and you must be Ms. Ruth, it's nice to meet you my name is Mya." I spoke with a smile and giving her eye contact the entire time. I took a moment to admire how beautiful she was, and baby was she beautiful, she didn't look a day over 35, the true definition of that old saying black don't crack.

"Good morning Ms. Draught, this is my mother Ruth, and mom this is Mya who I was telling you about, she's one of the nurses here." I reached my hand out to shake her and she pushed it away.

"We do hugs in my family, well if we get a good vibe." We both laughed and she gave me the tightest hug that reminded me of my mother. I stayed and talked to Ms. Ruth for a while until she felt a bit more comfortable, and I could already tell she would become one of my favorite residents.

It was finally time for me to clock out and head home, thoughts of going to the club were way behind me, all I wanted to do now was kick my feet up and relax, fuck the club!

As I was walking toward my car my phone began ringing, and I knew who it was before I even looked down at my phone, as soon as I pressed the answer button my best friends loud ass voice came booming through.

"Bitch, where you at?" Naya asked me sounding hyped as hell, I had to take a second to laugh at her crazy ass, what I loved most about my girl was she was crazy as hell.

"Just getting off work and now I'm about to head home." I rolled my eyes, because I knew she was about to go off about me not going to the club.

"Head home for what Mya? It's fine nigga Friday, so get dressed and I'll be at your house by 8:00, that's five hours for you to rest, shit, shower and whatever else you need to do. I already got our pre-game drinks, so ain't no turning back bih." She laughed and hung up; as much as my cousin irritated me I loved her crazy ass even more.

I shook my head because I knew damn well there was no canceling on Naya's ass, that girl stayed on go. When I got home I took a quick shower and picked out my clothes which looked exactly like it did in my head at work, I was wearing a crop top with blue jeans, that were cut out with chains on them starting at the thigh and some nude pumps. I put my hair into a messy bun with my baby hairs on fleek as they say.

I decided against make-up and chose natural beauty for tonight; I grabbed my phone to send Naya a text.

Me: Where you at?

Bestie: Parking bih, damn! I said 8 it's 7:50

As I was laughing at our dumb asses she was walking through the door with the liquor in hand, I grabbed the bottle of D'usse and grabbed two shot glasses from the shelf, and with that our pregame begun.

Markell

I was sitting at the bar with my brother shooting the shit when I saw Mya walk in; she looked beautiful as I took her in head to toe, all these women in the club but all I could see was her.

As she made her way to the bar she was stopped several times, and each time I got pissed off more and more. At one point a dude grabbed her by the waist and they danced. I stared at the way her hips moved, I imagined her throwing her legs across my shoulders and a smirk crept across my face. She continued to dance on him until she lifted her head and our eyes connected. I wanted to look away but I couldn't, she stared back at me as she mouth the lyrics to wild thoughts by DJ Khaled and Rihanna.

I don't know if you could take it

Know you wanna see me nakey, nakey, naked

I wanna be your baby, baby, baby

Spinning and it's wet just like it came from Maytag

White girl wasted on that brown liquor

When I get like this I can't be around you

I'm too lit to dim down a notch

'Cause I could name some thangs that I'm gon' do

I was in a trance as she danced and mouthed the words to me; my brother tapping me on my shoulder brought me out of my trance. "Yo, Markell, you good?" I looked away from Mya for a minute and toward my brother. "Yeah bro, I'm good." I got back in the conversation with my boys, but still kept my eyes on Mya.

It was about 30 minutes before the club was too closed and everyone started to disburse. I noticed Mya was so drunk she could barely stand. "Aye Malcolm, come give me a hand with these two." I yelled out to my brother. He took a few minutes to wrap up his conversation before coming to join me. "Bro you know these bitches, they drunk as fuck." I shook my head because I was too irritated. "Yeah, this is Mya, the nurse at mom's home that you grabbed when we moved her shit in."

My brother was becoming more and more irritated as we walked them toward our cars, because the friend kept stepping on his shoes. He let her ass go and the friend hit her ass hard as fuck on the ground, "Hell naw! This drunk bitch ain't giving my mom shit." He yelled loud as fuck, and began to draw attention to us.

"Man shut the fuck up Mac, niggas don't be saying they don't want your drunken ass making they beats do they?" I grilled his ass. "Matter of fact just go I'll call up Dre to help me."

"Man, just tell me where the fuck we taking they ass, so we can get this shit over with." He began to mumble some shit under his breath, but I wasn't stuntin his ass one bit. We finally made it to the car, Mya and her home girl were now snoring. "Bro, where we taking they ass, they knocked the fuck out and we don't know where the fuck they stay? I'm trying to go crawl up in something wet and preferably awake." He grabbed the girl hand and let it go as he spoke causing me to laugh at his dumb ass.

"Man let's take them to mom's spot to sleep this shit off, it ain't shit there to steal so they'll be good. He pondered on what I was saying before speaking.

"No, let's check they ID and take they ass to their own shit." I thought about what my brother was saying and went with his idea. We pulled up to Mya's house, and I was surprised that she only stayed about 10 minutes from me over in Santa Monica, right off the beach.

I grabbed her keys and opened up her door, it was a cool breeze inside. I turned on the light and shit I felt like I was at home; her décor was almost like mine, same couch and everything. I found her bedroom and politely undressed her, put her in bed and left out. When I got to the living room I saw Malcolm basically just threw that damn girl on the couch, her fucking legs were hanging off and everything. I shook my head as I locked her door and headed home, hard as fuck.

Mya

I woke up to the bright ass sun shining in my face, Looking around I saw I was home in my bra and panties in my guest room, but I couldn't remember getting here. I got up too see if anyone else was here and that's when I saw Naya ass laying on my damn couch, with half of her body hanging to the floor.

I smacked her on the ass hard as fuck, she jumped up quick. "Fuck Mya, you play too damn much." She yelled while rubbing her ass in the spot I just hit her in; I blew her a kiss and headed toward the kitchen to put on a pot of coffee. Naya came in and made us both omelets for breakfast. Once everything was done we tried to figure out how we got home. "Bitch, don't you still have that damn camera above your door your uncle made you get?"

"Damn Naya, I had forgotten all about that, I guess it's a good thing I tell your nosey ass everything." I went and got my laptop and pulled the app up. Once I logged in, I watched as Markell and his brother carried us in, and were gone not even five minutes later. I continued to watch as Markell stopped and looked into the camera, then winked at me. I swear just that action alone had my panties soaked.

I was kind of relieved, but at the same time embarrassed that he'd seen me that way; I was glad he cared enough to bring me home. Without thinking I logged into my company's website, and got his number off his mother's chart.

I sat there staring at his number wondering if I should call or not, and if I did what the hell would I say? I let out a frustrated sigh while closing the computer.

"If you're doing all that you might as well call the man, hell it don't get any weirder than him knowing where you stay without you telling him. Make the call Mya, don't overthink it." Then she walked off yelling, "Thank him for me too." I chuckled at her while trying to figure out if Naya was the angel or devil on my shoulder, but throwing caution to the wind I made the call.

"Hello?" His voice was deep and sexy as hell.

"Hey Markell, how are you? It's Mya, the nurse from Hope Memory Care." I said hoping he'd remember me.

"Oh what's up Ms. Mya, how's your head feeling?" I was turning red from embarrassment.

“It’s good, I had my morning cup of coffee, so I’ll be good. I just wanted to thank you for bringing us home.” Talking to him had my ass feeling like a teenager, pacing the living room and cheesing for no damn reason.

“I have another way you can thank me.” I stopped pacing to get serious with him for a minute.

“Oh yeah, and what way is that Markell?” I asked with a hint of attitude, I didn’t want him thinking I was that girl.

“You can treat me to dinner tonight at 8; I got a taste for steak so make it a steak house.”

“Steak, If I’m treating shouldn’t I get to pick the place?” I laughed as I said it because I never had to treat a man to dinner before.

“Usually yeah, but I make my own rules baby girl, that’s boss shit.” He stated so calmly and confidently that I not only believed it, I felt it.

“Alright then boss, text me your address and I’ll pick you up at 8.

Markell

As I got off the phone with Mya, my brother walked in. “Wassup bro?” I said as we slapped hands.

“Shit, ready to get this meeting over with, that nigga Jay got to go he been skimming money from the trap over on Budlong for about two months.” I could see the fire in his eyes as he spoke. That nigga Jay had been a problem since his brother got killed in a drive by, and we couldn’t find the shooter. Word on the street was, it was some personal shit about him fucking with some niggas baby mama, but we couldn't find any info on that.

I dragged my hand down my face, "How you want handle this?" I knew his answer before I even asked him.

"Today at the meeting let niggas know not to fuck with our shit!" He slammed his hand down on the desk. I nodded at my brother and we got ready to set shit off, to remind these niggas why we ran shit.

We left the office and headed over to the warehouse where the meeting was taking place, all our soldiers were already in attendance, everyone knew our slogan 'beat us there, don't meet us there'. We had the corner boys on one side and the Lieutenants on another, for the most part our team was thorough as fuck, aside from the issue we were now having with Jay. Our money was ready on time; our team handled all issues without us having to tell them what to do.

We walked in the warehouse and Mac spoke first. "Does anybody know why we had to call this meeting today?" We both looked around as no one spoke up.

I stepped in front of them, "Well let me tell you, someone has been skimming money from the house on Budlong for two months now, coming up to about 30,000 dollars." I walked by the flunkies that worked in that house and none of them showed an ounce of fear, but I didn't expect them to because we didn't have any pussies in our crew. "Do you want to tell us who it is, or do you want us to tell you which of you thieving muthafuckas thought it was okay to bite the hand that feeds you?"

Just when I was getting ready to speak Jay spoke up, "With all due respect Cash, none of the niggas that work over on Budlong skim anything, I can vouch for all of them and you've known me for 10 years." The more he spoke the angrier I got, because his bitch ass was the one stealing from us, putting the people under him in the position they were in now. "You right Jay, I've known your ass for years, but that didn't stop you from stealing from us did it?"

"Man you tripping Mac, I ain't stole shit in my life. I've always worked for everything I have and I make good ass money, so why would I steal from you?" The look on his face showed he was pissed and hurt that I asked.

"Everyone get out!" I yelled. I believed Jay, so we needed to get down to the bottom of this shit.

"Bro, what the fuck is you doing? We got this nigga on tape stealing from us, kill his ass and let's be done with this shit." Mac said getting pissed. I pulled up the video of Jay stealing the money and showed it to him, I watched him as he looked and I knew that look on his face was one of shame and disappointment.

"Mac and Cash, I swear that ain't me but I know who it is, I'm asking to be the one to handle it because –

Mac interrupted him "Hell naw you can't, nigga we ain't dumb we see you stealing the fucking money."

Jay sighed and rubbed his hand down his face, "It's my twin brother James, he got out of prison about four months ago and was begging to be put on, but the circumstances of him getting out was sketchy so I told him no." Me and Mac looked at each other dumbfounded we had forgotten all about James.

"Yo Jay, that's our bad, but you got to look at it from our point of view, you two are fucking identical." I shook my head, still unable to believe what the fuck I was hearing.

"Look Jay, you got 48 hours to handle it or we will, I know that's your brother so you can't kill him, but the money needs to be back in our pockets or that nigga will die." I walked off irritated as fuck for the day.

I chopped it up with my brother by the car for a minute about business and shit, then I headed home to get ready for my date with Mya, I sent her a text with my address since it was going on 7 o'clock, I got my shit ready for the shower to wash the bullshit of the day off me.

As I got out I went straight to the closet looking for something to wear, I decided on some black Balmain jeans and a grey button up with some grey loafers, damn I looked good as fuck. I sprayed my body with some of my Cuban cologne and I was ready to go.

Just as I was walking into the living room my phone went off with a message from Mya, saying she was outside. When I walked out the door I cracked the fuck up, because she was standing there outside the car with my door open like a straight nigga. She looked good in some white pants with a black half shirt that was made like a bra, and a white blazer on covering up her titties. Damn shorty was fly as fuck, and I knew she was about to turn a lot of heads tonight.

"Hey Ms. Mya, its good see you." I said as I licked my lips.

"It's good to see you as well Mr. Markell, are you ready for your steak?"

"I been ready for this muthafucka all day." We both laughed, I wasn't telling no lies my ass hasn't had shit to eat aside from some fucking frosted flakes at 10 this morning.

Mya

Shaking my thoughts away I reclined my seat to relax as I cruised down the highway. As I made my way down the 405 toward Redondo Beach I was in my zone, I had completely forgotten Markell was in the car because he was so quiet. I realized I wasn't alone as he laughed at my singing. I started to laugh until he joined in, and we vibed all the way to the restaurant rapping along to Future. 30 minutes and about 6 songs later we finally had pulled up to McCormick's Steakhouse, I swear I saw his mouth water, and as much as I wanted to crack I joke I decided to keep it cute for now.

I went to open my door and he popped my hand, as he got out the car to come open my door. "So, I see chivalry isn't dead with all men." He laughed at my statement and grabbed my hand. As were walking inside I couldn't help but think, damn a girl could get used to this. It took us about 5 minutes to be seated, while we were waiting Markell couldn't keep his hands off of me, so sitting down at the table was kind of a let down.

It had been so long since a man felt on me in any way, so his touch was setting off alarms all over my body. The waiter coming over to our table pulled me from my thoughts. "Welcome to McCormick's, I'm Desi and I'll be your waiter this evening. Can I start you off with some drinks?"

"Yes, I'll have a long island tea."

"And you sir?"

"Yes, I'll have an old fashioned." I laughed at his old ass drink order, because it was literally the shit that you see old ass men order in movies.

"Damn Ms. Mya, you just going to laugh at a nigga drink like that? What was I supposed to order, a martini or some girly shit like that? I could hear the humor in his voice as he spoke, which only made me laugh even more. "This a grown man drink Ms. Lady, it's what puts the hair on my chest." He slapped his chest for emphasis.

“If say so.” I shook my head as we finished our back and forth banter. About 10 minutes later the waiter was bringing our drinks and taking our order, I decided this was the perfect time to get to know him.

“So Markell, what is that you do for a living?”

“I do a lot, Real Estate and a few investments here and there, but my main business is in music. I own my own studio, alongside my brother. I write, produce shit you name it, I do it.”

He sounded so passionate as he spoke. “What got you into the music industry?”

“I mean look around, if our youth aren’t trying to play ball they trying be the next Pac or biggie so I figured why not help them along the way.” Listening to him speak was turning me on, the passion in his voice for his work mixed with the authority he commanded as he spoke had my kitty tingling.

“Mya!” I snapped out of my trance embarrassed as hell.

“Yes Markell?”

“The waiter asked if you’d like cheese on your salad.” He chuckled. I put my head down and said yes, ready to eat so he could divert his attention elsewhere.

Markell

The way Mya was staring at me just now I knew what she wanted, but now was not the time. Our conversation flowed so freely and I was feeling her ass, she was what niggas from the hood dreamed they women was like. She was smart, funny, beautiful and came with no baby daddy drama. She was a winner in my book. We finished our meal and I got the check, we argued on who was paying for a good 5 minutes until I won, but she still sat there with a pout. I took a good look at her pouting ass, and knew that she would be getting anything she wanted from me with very look.

On our way out the restaurant I got the keys and told her I would drive us home, she handed me the keys and was out before I even started the car. I drove us to my house and parked in the garage, I shut off the car and Mya hard sleeping ass was still out, snoring and all. I picked her up bridal style, while carrying her into my condo. The minute we walked in she was in awe, so I placed her on her feet so she could look around.

"Wow Markell, this is beautiful." She spoke as she dragged her finger across my counter tops.

"Thanks, my mom's helped me pick all this shit out." I watched her intently as she walked toward the bar and poured herself a small shot of Henny, and continued the tour around my place; she tried to open gun room but it was locked.

"Can I see what's in here, or is it private?" I thought long and hard about showing her, but then I said fuck it everything in here was registered and clean, I unlocked the door and held it open for her to walk in.

"Damn Markell, what are you a hitman?" She laughed at her own joke, and I just watched her admire my guns. She walked over to me slowly, seductively and from her drinks at the restaurant then the shot of Henny, I could tell she was feeling herself a bit, plus from what I could tell she was bad at holding her liquor.

"Should I take your silence as a yes Markell, Huh? Do you kill people?" Before I could answer her she kissed me, and it was deep as fuck. She jumped in my arms and was unbuttoning her blazer, taking it off when someone behind us cleared their throat.

"Hey Cash, What's going on here?" I could tell it was my housekeeper Asia, that I mess around with.

"What the fuck are you doing here Asia?" Mya tried to get out of my arms, but I kept a tight grip so her ass wasn't going anywhere.

"What you mean, why am I here? I fucking live here Cash." I let go of Mya so I could turn around, plus I couldn't take the look that was in her eyes. "You don't fucking live here Asia, you need to leave?" I knew it was about to be some shit by the smirk she gave me.

"So I don't live here? Well fuck it let me go to our room and get my shit out; I can't believe you really going to play me in front of this bitch." I walked up to Asia and hemmed her ass up by her collar, feet dangling above the ground an all. "Look Asia, I don't know what games you playing but I ain't the one." When I let her go I heard the front door slam, and it was then that I noticed Mya had walked out my place and was gone.

"Asia, get your shit and get the fuck out of my house, you're fired!"

Mya

I felt so fucking stupid on my way home; I never even asked him if he had someone in his life, so the fucking joke was on me. My phone started to ring, I looked down and saw that it was Markell, or Cash, whatever the fuck people were calling him; I ignored it and drove home.

I parked my car in the carport, so he would think I wasn't home and not come bothering me. My drunk ass would probably have given up the goodies, had that Barbie looking bitch not walked in when she did, I was really hurt low-key because I was feeling him with my foolish ass. Yes I know I didn't know him that long but whatever, when you know you fucking know.

My phone rang again and I finally answered "What Markell?" I asked him loudly, while trying to keep my composure together because part of me really wanted to cry.

"Let me come see you and make it up to you, I promise it's not what you think ma, just let me explain."

I pulled myself together and said three words, "I'm cool thug." Then proceeded to hang up the phone. I felt a sense of sadness rush over me, but better now rather than later. I showered and got ready for bed, I was over this day and ready to try again.

While sleeping I was awaken by a noise I swear sounded like glass breaking, I went to my closet and got my gun ready to kill somebody if need be. I walked toward the front of my house, checking around like I was the police on of these damn TV shows I need to quit watching.

When I got to my front door I saw a shadow, I shot and shot until I was being thrown toward the floor, I screamed and fought until something was put over my mouth. "Calm down Mya, it's me ma." I knew that was nobody but fucking Markell.

"What the fuck are you doing in my house?" I was beyond irritated and pissed that I just wasted some good bullets.

"I'm here because you wouldn't let me fucking explain damn, you about to take a nigga head the fuck off. Relax ma and chill out for a minute." He took the gun out my hands and put it behind his back. "What the fuck can you say that will fix what the fuck just happened? I looked like a damn fool when your bitch walked in there. We were like four kisses away from me fucking your brains out in your gun room." Looking at him I was getting turned on, and being mad just wasn't an option any more.

"I swear that wasn't my bitch, that was my crazy ass housekeeper, she ain't nothing to me she just clean my fucking house Mya. There is so many bitches out here that will try you if we talk ma, I need to know you won't always fold. I need to know that you here ma." He looked so sincere as he spoke. "The way you pulled that gun out was sexy as fuck ma … You the one and you don't even know it."

I looked him in his eyes as he spoke and I believed him, I also saw something in his eyes that seemed to be begging me to believe him. I walked closer to him and kissed him roughly, and the next thing you know we were going at it, he slammed me against every wall on the way to my bedroom, I'm guessing to make sure I knew who was running shit, but little did he know I liked it. "I like that rough, shit Cash." Calling him Cash seemed to trigger something in him, because he got way more aggressive.

He threw me on the bed and looked me dead in my eyes "Take those fucking pants off Mya, Now!" I wasn't scared but I was fucking intrigued, and I definitely wanted to know this Cash person.

I took off my pants and was about to take off my bra but he told me to stop. "Come here ma, just like that." I did as he said and walked over to him, he picked me up and I wrapped my legs around his waist and hungrily kissed him. "Tell me you want me Mya." I stopped kissing him and looked him dead in his eyes as I said the words he wanted to hear, "I want you."

When I said those words gone was the aggressive Cash, and back was the passionate Markell, he laid me down and kissed from my neck to my stomach, on my thighs and as he went further down he began to tug at my underwear. He flicked my clitoris with his tongue teasing me with anticipation and making me want more. "Fuck Markell, I can't take it baby, do it." He laughed at me, and I probably would have laughed too if I wasn't horny as hell.

Finally giving in to my begging, he began to feast on pussy like it was a full Thanksgiving meal; I had never experienced something so magnificent in my whole life.

When he finished he stood over me, never breaking eye contact which I was learning was a big thing for him, he pulled down his pants and I swallowed the lump that was forming in my throat. Yes, I have gotten head before, yes I'd given head before but I never had sex before. Guessing that he could sense my uneasiness I kissed him and pulled his face into mine, just as we was about to put the head in his phone rung. Fuck my life.

Markell

Hearing my burner phone go off I knew that shit had to have been an emergency, if not I was killing whoever the fuck was interrupting shit. Looking down at Mya, I saw her asking me with her eyes not to answer it, but I had to.

"Speak." I listened to Mac tell me that one of traps was hit this afternoon, and two of our foot soldiers had gotten hit. "Fuck, which one?"

"Budlong bro, the fucking trap on Budlong." When he said that I knew it couldn't be anybody else but Jay's pussy ass brother.

“Alright say less I’m on my way, give me about 15 minutes.” We said our goodbyes and hung up. I grabbed my phone and called Jay.

“What’s up boss?” He sounded groggy like I woke him up, but I didn’t give a fuck.

“Budlong, 15 minutes, beat me there.” I hung up the phone and Mya was standing there in her robe mugging me. I ran my hand down my face, because I was truly fucking shit up when it came to dealing with this girl.

“So that’s why she called you Cash? You’re a fucking drug dealer?” I was stunned and trying to figure out how she got that from anything I said, as if reading my mind she continued. “Your brother voice is very loud, I heard him say something about a trap and some people being murdered.” I didn’t have time to explain shit to her so I grabbed my jeans, stepped in them and went to the bathroom to rinse my mouth out, wasn’t no other nigga about to know what my girl’s pussy smelled like.

When I came out the bathroom I didn’t see her in the room, so I walked around looking for her and I finally found her mean ass, holding the fucking door open for me to get out her shit.

Right before I walked out she grabbed me. “Can I have my fucking gun back?” I laughed at her because her ass looked gangster ass fuck asking for her shit.

I kissed her on her cheek before responding, “Nah.” With that I proceeded out the door like the cocky ass nigga I was.

***

When I pulled up to the trap on Budlong, I tried to calm myself because at this moment I was beyond fucking pissed. In all the years we had been running shit no one has come at us on no rah rah shit like this nigga James was now.

To make matters worse he looked exactly like that nigga Jay, so our young niggas felt they could trust him. I ran my hand through my waves and walked toward the house, when I walked inside both my brother and Jay were already there.

"How much we get hit for?" I wasn't asking anybody directly, yet nobody said shit. "Somebody in this muthafucka better speak. Fast!" I took my gun out and cocked it back ready to shoot everybody in this fucking room.

"Sixty thousand dollars and a couple of bricks." The youngest nigga in here was the one to answer my question.

I was beyond furious and ready to shoot Jay ass, just for looking like his pussy ass brother. "Jay from here on out you are not allowed in any of the traps without me or Mac, simply because you and your brother are fucking twins, secondly your ass is paying for both of those niggas funerals." Jay hung his head down as I spoke, but I was speaking facts and there really wasn't shit he could say.

"Another thing, Jay we are killing your brother on site." I walked out the trap to let that shit marinate for a minute, and headed home to lay my ass down because shit was getting hectic as fuck.

Despite all of the bullshit I went through I actually got some pretty good sleep, so I woke up called up my people and had some of our traps moved around, I no longer wanted the nigga with the code to the safe serving, so I was about to come up with a whole new system. Niggas could break in the house and go against my soldiers, but they were walking out empty fucking handed because no one there would access the money.

After handling my business, I had a few free hours to spare, I decided to go see my leading lady. On my way to my mom's facility, I stopped and grabbed her favorite movie to watch with her and some popcorn.

Once I was all signed in and going to her room I could hear voices. "Oh Ms. Ruth you are a mess, I swear you're going to become my favorite resident." I knew that was Mya.

"Oh hush child, I'm already your favorite." They both giggled at my mom's admission.

"I will admit you do keep me on my toes with your shenanigans."

"See, now tell me about Mya, we always up in my business trying to get me to take those god forsaken pills, the least you could do is tell me about yourself." My mom was always nosey as fuck, so I wasn't surprised at her asking that.

"It's really not much to tell Ms. Ruth, I had a great life until about 8 years ago when I turned 16. My mother died of a drug overdose and my father was killed right in front of me, I then lived with my uncle and his wife until my 18th birthday, I went to college and now I'm here." I could hear the tears in her voice.

"Oh hunny I am so sorry, I never would have asked had I known. If ever you need to talk or need some motherly advice I'm here, I may not remember everything tomorrow but I am here today nonetheless." They hugged it out, I felt bad for intruding and eavesdropping on a private moment so I knocked.

"Hey mom, I came to spend the day with you, hey Mya." I hugged my mom first and then went to try and hug Mya, but she curved the fuck out of my ass.

“Hey son, what you bring me.” She asked as she snatched the bag out of my hand.

“Titanic, oh yes let me use the restroom and I’ll be ready son.” She winked at me as she spoke; my mom was a class act with dementia and all.

“Mya, I missed you.” I grabbed her and held on to her, inhaling the scent that I had begun to love.

“I missed you Cash.” She said my name as if it disgusted her, and that shit was new to me, bitches would usually be throwing their panties at the hood legend that was Cash.

“Look, you can be pissed I didn’t tell you, but let’s be real that’s not something you just rush to tell someone.” I grabbed her chin and made her look at me. I knew she understood where I was coming from, but she still felt a little betrayed.

She was about to speak but there was a knock on the door, so I let her go and gave her some room since this was her place of work. “Hey Mya, can I speak with you in my office for a second.” Some square ass black dude said. I could see him undressing Mya right in front of me.

She was about to walk off when I spoke, “Can it wait a second, we were discussing my mother’s medication.” He nodded and walked off.

“Are you fucking that nigga?” I asked her point blank and she better hope the answer was no.

She rolled her eyes, “No Markell, I’m not. We went on a few dates and that’s it.” I was satisfied with her answer, so I let her go after kissing her on the lips and smacking her on her ass. Damn that girl.

Mya

Damn, I was so pissed at myself for being weak for that nigga. The fucked up part was him being a drug dealer was kind of a turn on. I always wanted to date a bad boy, but my uncle wasn't going for it. After I while I just said fuck it, and went for the square and safe type.

Walking toward Marshall's office I got annoyed, me and Marshall went on a few dates, nothing about him excited me. He dressed preppy, kind of like Carlton from the *Fresh Prince of Bel Air* and I hated that, I at least thought he would step it up for our dates but nope, he couldn't even do that.

I knocked on his door before opening it, "Yes Marshall, what did you need to speak to me about?" I watched him watch me, and it was very uncomfortable.

"I need to speak with you about Ms. Ruth, she has been here for a few days now and she is giving all of our nurses a hard time except you, now would you like to tell me why that is?" He stood up out of his chair and walked toward me, placing his hand on my shoulder.

"I just am good at my job Marshall, your nurses as well as caregivers are here for a paycheck and that's it, you need to give lessons on going above and beyond. Then maybe she'll open up to them, but I'll also start to accompany other nurses and show them the correct way to care for her." He began to massage my shoulders and I felt uncomfortable. "If there isn't anything else though I need to finish med pass."

"Nope that'll be all ... Oh and Mya, remember we have a policy against dating family of residents here. I rolled my eyes and countered him.

"Marshall, remember we have a policy against dating coworkers, and I'm pretty sure that massage you just gave me was considered sexual harassment, so stay the fuck in your lane." I slammed his door and went to my office.

A few hours later and I was ready to go home, just as I locked up my office I turned around and walked head first right into Markell.

"You good ma, did that fuck boy say something to you?" His brows furrowed as he spoke about Marshall.

"No, not really, he was just reminding me of our policy against dating family of the residents." I chuckled as I spoke because he really had some nerve.

"We good, so look what you got planned for the night?" I didn't really have anything planned, but I be damned if I told him that.

"I'm going out for drinks with my bestie Naya and her dude, then home, why you want to join?" I asked being funny I had no way his dumb ass would say yes.

"Yeah I'll come, I'll meet you at your house around let's say around 8pm?" I nodded and he grabbed my face and kissed me hard before leaving. When I looked up there was Ms. Ruth.

"I knew you would be the perfect match for my son, don't let him run over you though. You will have to put my son in his place, hell slap his ass if you have to. My son's are reserved when it comes to women, they aren't willingly giving up there heart babygirl." We talked a bit more until she kissed me on my head and went our separate ways.

***

I was finally dressed and look like a whole fucking meal, fuck a snack I was killing bitches tonight. I was wearing an all black mini dress that had my back cut out as well as my sides, I decided on some black Louboutins. Deciding on what to do with my hair, I put it up in a messy bun with baby doll bangs, I beat my face with a natural look and damn did I look good. I through some diamond hoops in my ear and was ready to go. I made it all the way to the door before doubling back to my room because I forgot the most important part, perfume. I sprayed myself down with *My Burberry Black* and was now ready to go.

I drove all the way to Naya house listening to *Bodak Yellow by Cardi B*, I was rapping along with her like this was my song, especially the part coming up:

I don't bother with these hoes, don't let these hoes bother me

They see pictures, they say, "Goals," bitch, I'm who they tryna be

Look, I might just chill in some BAPE , I might just chill with your boo

I might just feel on your babe, my pussy feel like a lake

He wanna swim with his face, I'm like, "Okay"

I'll let him get what he want, he buy me Yves Saint Laurent

I rapped that shit all the way to Naya house and it was just going off as I pulled up, I hopped out the car and knocked on her door before remembering she don't lock shit, as I walked in I heard noise in the living room so that's where I headed.

"Naya, I'm here. Now hurry up before we be, aaaaagh Naya, Jay what the fuck man?" I screamed out seeing my bestie get fucked was a sight I never wanted to see again, and I knew I would be scared for life.

"Mya! What the fuck, when did you get here?" Naya asked as she laughed, I was completely mortified and ready to take my ass home.

"I got here like 5 minutes ago, ugh just hurry up and wash your funky ass so we can go." I grabbed my phone to text Markell, letting him know what club. It took Naya and Jay ass 20 minutes to get cleaned up, and we were heading out.

When we pulled up to this banging ass club in Malibu called *323* and that shit was live, Jay had scored us a booth and we were getting wasted as fuck, Jay kept the bottle service coming all night and lord knows I needed it after dealing with Marshall and Markell. I had been here for two hour and no sign of Markell, so I decided to go out to the dance floor and let loose.

As soon as I stepped foot on to the dance floor I felt the liquor plus my song came on which was wild thoughts, I felt this guy come up behind me and start grinding into me so I danced back into him, I turned around and he wasn't too bad looking either so I continued. After about 4 or 5 songs I was exhausted and was walking off when he grabbed me by my waist, I usually would have cussed him out, but the liquor had me gone.

"You running off little momma, stay and have a drink with me." His offer sounded good, but I declined.

"I'm here with my friends, but maybe later." I tried to back away and he wouldn't let me go. "Let me the fuck go, now." His eyes were dark and he looked possessed. I tried to get away from him but it was no use, and in Cali people would turn away before helping you out. That was my last thought before I was hit in the head with something hard.

When I came to we were out of the club and close to his car, I fought and kicked, hell I even screamed but there was obviously no help coming for me, so I had to save myself. "Why are you doing this? If it's about money, I have money you can have it." I felt him poke me in the back with something and by the feel of it I knew it was a gun, I was not about to die in some fucking parking lot like a fucking hood cliché no ma'am, not Mya. I turned around and stared at him for a while before I leaped and we began to wrestle for the gun, until finally POP! POP! POP!

Markell

Finally arriving to the club, I knew I was going to hear Mya's mouth because she texted me over an hour ago, but business took forever.

I walked in an scanned the building looking for her, until I saw her home girl I went to ask her where Mya was.

"What's up little momma, where your girl at?" It was weird as fuck because some nigga was sucking on her neck so she finally pushed him away. Me and dude locked eyes and I was laughing my ass off "Jay, what's up bro. This you?" I asked pointing at oh girl.

"Yeah bro, this my girl Naya, Naya this my bro Cash." He introduced us and we shook hands. She told me Mya went to go dance and I immediately got hot, thinking about some nigga trying to feel up on what was mine. I looked around the dancefloor but I didn't see her, so I went to check the restroom and she wasn't there either.

I decided to see if she signed her death certificate and took one of these niggas out back, and as soon as I got out there I saw her standing far as fuck by some cars. "Mya, why you all the way over there, no fuck that ma why you outside? It better not be no nigga over there for his sake and yours." I stopped talking because the closer I got I saw that Mya killed a nigga outside of a crowded ass nightclub, bloody as fuck and still holding the smoking fucking gun.

I walked up to her, “Mya, baby give me the gun and go to my car, don’t talk to anybody and don’t stop for anything.” She was just staring at him and not paying me any attention, “Mya, go now.” She finally snapped out of it and took my keys, hauling ass to my car.

Shaking my head I took out my phone and called Jay from out the club and the cleanup crew. “Cash, why the fuck you paging me 911 what’s going on?” He stopped talking as he saw this nigga lying here dead as fuck.

“Please tell me you ain’t kill this nigga for dancing with Mya short ass?” He was laughing as he spoke, but I wasn’t telling this nigga what the fuck just happened and that was for damn sure.

“No nigga, fuck him right now, I need you to go in the club and get the fucking security tapes and bring them bitches to me, and I need them like now Jay.” Sensing the urgency in my voice he turned his ass around quick and went to do what I asked his ass to do.

Half an hour later Mac and the cleanup crew finally arrived, I watched as they swiftly cleaned up the blood and got his body the fuck out of there. I told they ass to make sure it couldn’t be found, and if for whatever reason it is make sure it can’t be identified. I decided to get rid of the gun myself, I be damned if my future wife was caught up, so I couldn’t trust nobody to handle that shit besides myself.

Finally making it back to the car I saw Mya, laying in my front seat in nothing but her bra so I’m assuming she came up out that bloody dress, *smart girl*. I took my shirt off and gave it to her, she didn’t speak as she put it on and I wasn’t going to force it yet, so I hopped in my ride and drove us to my house.

I decided to run her some bath water so she could relax and put her mind on other things. "Mya, come get in your bath." She slowly stood up and came out of my shirt and her under clothes, damn her body was a thick work of art. I had to mentally tell myself not right now, because looking at her right now had me ready to fuck her six ways to Sunday.

"Markell, tell me exactly what it is you do?" I sat on the floor next to the tub as she got comfortable and waited for me to speak.

"Ma, we can talk about this later."

"Have you killed people before Markell?" I wore a blank expression as she tried to read me.

"I've killed a lot of people Mya, I don't regret it and if I had to kill them again I would." She nodded as if she understood.

"Do you enjoy it?" I don't know where the fuck that question came from, but I answered her truthfully.

"Yes, I do. If they cross me or pose a threat, I will eliminate it no questions asked ma, but that comes with that line of work I'm in." Again she just nodded.

"I think I enjoyed killing him tonight, I wasn't in shock because of what just happen. I was in shock because I liked the way it felt, I felt powerful. He tried to rape me Markell, he wanted to take something from me, but instead I took something from him and I liked it." I knew she meant that shit because I felt the intensity of her words, and after she spoke them she washed herself off as if the whole conversation never happened.

I was looking at Mya in a new light, not only was she smart, sexy and funny, but she was about to be my wife and my rider. I was sitting in my study sipping on some Henny when Mya walked in wearing nothing but a towel, and it dawned on me I forgot to grab her something to sleep in. “Markell?”

“Yeah ma, what’s up?” I looked up at her giving her my undivided attention.

She dropped her towel and said, “Make love to me.”

Mya

I said it just above a whisper but he still heard me, he picked me up bridal style and carried me toward his bedroom. He looked me in my eyes the whole time; he laid me down gently and gave me a trail of kisses starting from my neck to my chest.

“Oooh Markell, don’t stop.” I moaned, it was almost desperate like. He continued his kisses down to my breast, and played with my navel with his tongue.

“You like that baby? Tell daddy you like that feel.” He hummed on my clit as he spoke to me.

“Yes daddy, I love that way that feels, oh god don’t stop.” He licked and slurped until I was trying to push his head away. “Fuck, Cash I’m about to cum.” I was having an outer body experience.

“Let it go baby, let that shit go Mya. Give it to me.” As if he spoke the magic words I came all over his face and in his mouth. “Damn you taste good as fuck.” He said as he mounted me, kissing me. He stood up and took off his clothes. I swallowed the large lump that was forming in my throat, because good lord baby was hung. He had to be at least a good 10 or 11 inches, and I just always knew my first time would be with a nigga was maybe 7 or 8, you know the average dick size.

He was back on top of me kissing me, and as he put his dick near my entrance I stopped him.

"I've never done this before, please be gentle." He looked conflicted, like he didn't want to anymore so I kissed him, "I want this baby, with you." I gave him the confirmation he needed and he began working the head in. My reflexes were to tighten my legs so I did and grabbed around his neck very tightly.

"Baby you got to loosen up. I promise to be as gentle as possible." I nodded and loosened up my legs and arms. He kissed me deeply as he pushed and I screamed into his mouth, it hurt so fucking badly for the first few strokes, but once I got used to his size and just sex period I was matching his strokes.

"Oh you feeling it now huh ma, turn that ass around." As I was doing as I was told, he smacked me on my ass hard as fuck as we went at it all night.

"You felt that girl, that was my son I just gave you." We both laughed and snuggled up to go to sleep.

One Year Later…

"Hey boss Lady, is Cash around?" I rolled my eyes because I was so fucking annoyed by Jay's voice, ever since he stopped fucking around with Naya he'd changed, hell one day he actually asked me what my name was which was odd as fuck seeing how we had known each other for years.

"No Jay, he isn't here if you need him call him, don't pop up over here no more, if you need to reach Cash then you need to call him and find his ass." I slammed the door and went back to the room to find me some scrubs for work.

Me and Markell have been rocking heavy since everything went down at the club that night; there weren't any more secrets between us, I had started helping Markell out with his "business" just the small things, I would do pickups here and there or drop money off to the families of people in his crew who wouldn't be returning home.

Most people would call me Lady Cash or Boss Lady, but I really just preferred to be called Mya, plain ole Mya. Pulling my phone out I called Markell.

"What's up babe, why you not at work with your big headed ass?" I laughed at his corny ass.

"Shut up fool, my head is perfectly round thank you, and I'm walking out the house now to go to Starbucks. I just wanted to let you know Jay popped up over here looking for you again." He sighed and I could clearly here the irritation in his voice.

"I'll handle it babe, that nigga know damn well not to pop up at the crib, on the real though I've been thinking about getting us a new spot. Too many people know where we lay our heads at night and that ain't a good look, you feel me." I nodded as if he could see me.

"Cool, I'm with that. I'll call up my realtor and see if we can see a few places this week, what's you budget with your cheap ass?" He smacked his lips at me.

"Now your brown skin ass know ain't nothing about me cheap, just enough room for us to think about starting our family." Okay babe, I'm at Starbucks I'll hit you on my break, and yes I'll tell mom you said hi."

"Good looking out ma, I love you."

"I love you too babe."

Markell

Hanging up with Mya I focused back on the task at hand, "Stand that nigga up Mac, he need to be taught a lesson." We were at out warehouse beating the shit out of this nigga for trying to rob one of my traps.

"So you thought it was okay to steal from me little nigga?" I asked him, as I beat his ass with some metal chains we had laying around. He mumbled something but it wasn't audible. "Speak up little nigga I can't hear you." He coughed a little bit and my patience was wearing thin, right as I was about to hit him again he talked.

"He told me to do it, my mom's was sick and he paid us five grand each to do it, I'm not the only one. They plan to hit each of your traps every week." He coughed up blood and I knew we were losing him.

"Who paid you?" I grabbed him by his throat and put my ear close to his mouth, as he said the name I never thought I would be hearing again.

"James."

I dropped his ass right there in a pile of blood and walked to my office with my brother trailing me. "Who'd he name?" I ran everything down to him and he was beyond pissed. I grabbed my phone to call Jay and I didn't get an answer. I pushed everything off my desk in frustration. "I don't want him allowed access to any of traps, I want all the burners switched out and I want the traps rotated to the backup houses we have off of Rampart switched over to the houses on Normandie today, I don't want no product or money being taken and no soldiers dying." My brother nodded and went out to give the order, I was beyond drained and just ready to lay up in Mya for the rest of the night.

I decided to go check up on my mom's and go see Mya at work, she liked that mushy shit. After pulling up and checking in I went to Mya's office, she wasn't there, so I just headed to check on my mom.

"Hey ma."

"Hey baby, what you doing here?" I walked closer in the room to hug her and we sat down.

"Damn ma, I didn't know I needed a reason to come see my number one lady anymore." I put my hand over my heart as if I was hurt.

"Shut up fool, you know your ass is always busy, if my daughter didn't work here I'd probably never see her ass either." I cracked up laughing at my mom, she always been a firecracker and a manipulator, but to know her is to love her.

We chopped it up for a few more minutes, I got up to go to the bathroom and when I was about to walk out Mya came running in the room in tears, so I decided to stay in the bathroom and eavesdrop.

"I can't do this no more momma Ruth, I just can't. I've tried staying as long as I could, but I have to leave before I kill his ass." My mother just held her as she cried.

"Look baby I know you just staying here for me, but I'll be fine you can go on and I'll still be okay." She looked up at my mom and laughed.

"Now momma Ruth, you know I ain't worried about you, I'm worried about you beating these nurses asses the minute I walk out that door." They shared a laugh and my mom kissed her on the cheek and she left out.

"Bring your eavesdropping ass out here." I laughed as I walked out.

"You two keeping secrets from me momma, I'm supposed to be your baby?"

"You know I always wanted a daughter, plus she sneaks me extra snacks from the kitchen." I laughed at mom but got serious.

"For real ma, what's going on with my girl? Somebody up here fucking with her I got that part, but who?" She shook her head no and stood up.

"Nope, I'm not getting in that, she told me in confidence and I will not break her trust, not even for my baby." I respected the bond they had, but right now that shit was irritating. I kissed my mom goodbye and headed to Mya's office.

"Hey babe, what you in here doing?" I could tell she had been crying her face was puffy and eyes were red.

She stood up to come hug me, "Hey baby, I'm just typing up a specific plan for the nurses here to deal with your mom, and you know she can be difficult. When I'm not here she refuses to allow anyone to give her medication."

"Yeah, she doesn't like these bitches up here, you quitting or some shit?" I looked her in the eyes to see what she was thinking.

"Yeah, I want to just relax for a minute then go back to school, I won't be living off of you bae I swear, I have some money saved and my trust is still untouched basically, so I'll be set for a few years." She rambled and fidgeted with her hands as she talked, my baby was nervous as fuck.

"You know I'm not worried about you living off of me, if I got it you got it and babe, I got it so relax." I held her as she melted in my arms. "Let's go home, you cooking for a nigga tonight, or should I stop and grab us something to eat?" She laughed and said to grab some Chinese, so I will do just that on the way home.

Mya

I was beyond pissed, Marshall's ass had passed me up for yet another promotion because I was dating Markell. Then on top of that he asked me if I was willing to do some personal things for him, that would have him consider me for a promotion. I worked my ass off harder than any of those nappy headed bitches at my job. Plus why would I fuck him for something that wasn't even guaranteed?

I was lying in bed with Markell, and I just couldn't shake the thought of killing his dumb ass. I got up and went to Markell's study and grabbed one of those extra burner phones he had, then called Marshall.

"Hello?" He sounded sleep but I knew his ass was about to wake right up.

"Hey Marshall, its Mya." I tried to sound interested and sexy, but right now the only emotion I was feeling was annoyance.

"Hey Mya, I didn't recognize the number. What's got you calling so late?"

“Well, I was thinking about what you said, about those personal things and I would like to take you up on your offer.”

“Really, right now?” He sounded giddy as fuck, and I wanted to laugh at his corny ass.

“Yes right now, unless you’re not interested anymore.” I rolled my eyes because I was over this whole conversation.

“No, I’m very interested, you remember my address from the Christmas party last year?”

“Yeah I remember, I’ll be there soon.” I hung up the phone, went to the room and threw on some black tights, a black hoodie and my timberlands, I was about to make Marshall wish he never gave me a fucking ultimatum. I grabbed my keys and was halfway out the room when Markell stirred, when I didn’t see him sit up and continued out the door.

Pulling up to Marshall’s house I knocked on his door and he opened it quick, damn he was thirsty as fuck.

“Hey Mya, you got here fast.”

“Some things can’t wait.” I said as I walked inside. “I really want that promotion, so tell me what exactly I have to do.” I said walking up on him seductively.

“Y-you h-have t-to umm, woo it’s hot in here.” I had to really hold my fucking laugh in as his stuttering ass couldn’t even get his words out, how fucking pathetic. “Mya, come back here hunny.” I rolled my eyes, then went to the back where he was laid out in the bed looking a plum fool. “I want to fuck you Mya.” He licked his lips hungrily and tried to touch me, but I smacked his hand away.

"No, close your eyes I have a surprise for you." He looked at me hesitantly, but did as I asked; I bent down to my shoe and pulled my gun out. "Open them." He opened his eyes and looked like he was about to shit on himself.

"Mya w-what are you doing? We can talk about this; the promotion is yours we had already voted on it." Him saying that pissed me off even more.

"Fuck your promotion and fuck that job." I shot him twice in the head, thanks to Markell and his ridiculous shooting range dates, I was basically a pro. After my common sense came back I realized I had no idea what I was going to do with his damn body. Thinking on my feet I decided to set his perverted ass on fire, along with this old ass house in the middle of fucking nowhere. I looked around for an accelerant and found some lighter fluid, I poured it all over his body and started a trail from the back of the house to the front, and even through some on the blinds.

I got a match and lit that muthafucka up, now I just had to get the fuck out of dodge. "Sayonara Marshall, and I hope you burn in hell."

Markell

Now I don't know why Mya's ole sneaky ass thought I wouldn't find out about what she did to that fuck boy Marshall, I wasn't mad that she did it, I was mad she didn't tell me. I was pissed that she did such a good job at covering her tracks, and even more pissed that she hasn't told me.

She been walking around here cleaning and humming, her ass don't hum, it took me back to that night she admitted that she enjoyed killing. I had to shake my head and figure out a way to get her to tell me. It had been two weeks too long, her ass better get to singing like a fucking canary and it better be good.

As I was getting ready to talk to her my phone rang, and it was my connect Ruiz.

"Ruiz, what's good?"

"Hola Cash, How is everything?" I could tell he was smoking one of those good ass Cubans.

"Everything is everything; to what do I owe the pleasure of this call?"

"Well, I have some business that needs to be discussed in person, how soon can you make it out here?" I thought for a minute and said. "I'll be on my way tonight." We never said goodbyes, so that was the end of the call.

Since Mya been on some bullshit lately, I wasn't taking her unless she told me what went down.

"Babe! Where you at?" I yelled looking for her, when I finally found her she was getting dressed. "Where the fuck are you going Mya?" She looked at me like I had grown two heads up in this muthafucka.

"First off watch how the fuck you talk to me, and secondly we have an appointment with my realtor to go look at some houses today, or did you forget?" She had a smirk on her face, while I was sitting there looking dumb as fuck.

"That's cool; well I'm leaving the country for a minute so Malcolm, will come check on you from time to time, just to make sure you good." I walked off after saying that.

"Why can't I go Markell? Where are you going? Who's going with you? How long will you be gone?" She fired off so many damn questions I didn't know which to answer first.

"You want to go bae?"

"Yes Markell, I want to go, it can be a baecation." She giggled as she said that because she knows I hate that fucking word.

"Tell me where you went that night you left out of here while I was asleep?" Tell me why you quit working and you can go."

"Markell, that's nothing babe."

"So you just going to keep lying to me, alright then I'll see you in three weeks." I was bluffing, I knew my ass would be back in four days, five tops but I would stay at a fucking hotel before I told the truth.

"Fine Markell, I was passed up for three promotions at work by Marshall because I was with you and I wouldn't fuck him. He told me to meet him at his house to fuck, except there was no fucking." I looked at my girl face and she didn't give one fuck, two fucks or a got damn blue fuck.

I hugged her tightly and whispered in her ear, "Next time you tell me, we can conqueror the muthafuckin world together baby, and I'm here for you. If you want a nigga handled fuck it he got to go, simple as that. Now go pack a bag, we're going to Colombia." She squealed with excitement, on one our many nights of pillow talk she told me her mom was Colombian, so I knew she would really enjoy this.

I sent a message to the realtor telling him we had a last minute family emergency that couldn't wait, fuck I was going to miss my condo, but moving was for the best so fuck it.

Pulling up to the airport we headed toward the private strip where they kept the private jets and shit, and Mya ass was staring at the side of my face crazy as fuck. "Baby didn't you tell me we have a jet. Do you know how many vacations I would have gone on by now?"

I was laughing at her crazy ass, but she was really pouting so I rubbed her thigh and apologized, "My bad ma, we'll go on plenty vacations after this one, is that cool?" She acted like she was thinking, but I saw the answer in her eyes whether she answered or not.

"Baby what part of Colombia are we going to?"

"Stop being so nosey girl and enjoy the flight." She rolled her eyes at me and picked up that damn kindle, I know one thing if her ass got to screaming out '*Oh my god that's bae'* I was throwing that shit against a fucking wall.

It took us about 7 hours, but we were finally landing in Bogota. Our driver was already on the tarmac waiting for us to step out, so there was no wait and I was happy about that, a nigga needed a fucking shower after two fucking minutes in this heat.

Mya

Once we landed in Bogota I felt so close to my mother, I felt like this was a trip we would have made together. My mom always talked about her favorite little brother, and if this wasn't a last minute trip I would have tried to find him.

My mother's family disowned her for marrying black, so I never met anyone on her side of the family.

"Babe, you good?" Markell asked with a concern look on his face.

"Yeah, I'm good just was having a moment." He grabbed my hand in understanding and we were headed to our hotel. We arrived at the Casa Medina, which was a part of the Four Seasons chain of hotels and I fell in love, it was built like a marvelous cathedral. Walking inside to the lobby the ceiling to floor length paintings were absolutely beautiful, there was a grand spiral staircase and a huge chandelier in there as well. The front desk was made out of old oak which was beautiful as well, but I was afraid to lean on or touch it. Once we were checked in we headed up to our suite, which of course was the entire 5th floor.

"Baby how fucking much are you spending on this?" I had to ask because it was breath taking; everything was decorated in white and brown. The couches were leather, and although they were beautiful they looked uncomfortable as fuck to sit on. There were abstract paintings throughout the room, and as I listened to my heels clink across the floor I knew we were walking on real fucking marble. "Baby we're walking on marble floors, I want these in our new house." He just laughed at me as he got out some clothes to shower.

"Girl stop acting like your ass ain't never seen marble floors."

"I haven't, nigga we have regular ass floors stop fronting Markell." We both just laughed.

As I walked toward the bathroom, I stopped when I saw the big ass fish bowl tub, I immediately started running water and took off my clothes, fuck a meeting my ass was about to soak.

"Really babe, you couldn't wait for a nigga?" I stood up out the tub and let him see my naked body, "You are always free to join me." Without needing me to say another word he stripped out of his clothes like his ass was on fire, as I laughed at him. He kissed me passionately right before he made love to me, rough love if that makes sense.

"Harder daddy, fuck me harder." Between my moans and the water splashing we were in our zone, we forgot all about the driver downstairs waiting on us as we made rough passionate love.

"Fuck Mya, I'm about to cum baby,"

"Cum for me baby. Yes right there." Just as we came there was a knock on the door, Markell went to answer it, I let the water out the tub and jumped in the shower for a quick wash up. Markell quickly joined me and we were getting dressed, and on our way out.

As we walked down the spiral staircase I admired Cash, I never called him Cash, but Markell was back in Cali and Cash was definitely in Colombia. He was wearing a crisp white linen suit, while I wore a white sheer dress with a lime green bikini underneath. We complimented the hell out of each other.

The ride to whomever we were meeting estate was almost an hour long, but the scenery was absolutely beautiful, the grass was green there was people working out in the fields and flowers as well as trees everywhere.

Pulling up to the estate I felt like his home was its own damn city, it was massive. It looked like the white house in DC but better, I didn't see any guards but I knew they were lurking somewhere around this muthafucka.

Markell and I got out the car and walked toward the door, but before we could knock it was being opened. "Senor Cash, we have been expecting you, right this way." The lady led us two separate ways, me toward a living room and Cash toward what looked like a study. "Cash, will be out in a minute, can I offer you some refreshments?" Her accent was thick and almost hard to understand, so I nodded at her with a smile and she disappeared.

I began looking at all the pictures on the wall of his family and they were all similar in resemblance. The maid brought me a glass of wine as I continued to admire his family. When I got to a huge photo above the fireplace, the glass slipped from my hands as I stared into the eyes of my mother.

Markell

"Cash long time my friend, how have you been?" We shared a brief hug and took our seats, Ruiz offered me a Cuban and I accepted.

"So what brings me here Ruiz, we never meet unless it's important." I watched his mannerisms as he smiled at me.

"Si my friend, I have brought you here for a proposition, I am getting old and ready to retire and I want you to take my place." To say I was shocked would be an understatement, I knew me and Ruiz was cool but damn.

"That sounds like one hell of a proposition Ruiz, but what's the catch?" By the look on his face I knew some bullshit was about to come from his mouth.

"As you know I have no sons, only daughters, and I need to be able to ensure their safety." It sounded good so I nodded my head; I could do that no problem.

"Of course I could make sure your daughters are safe."

"You must be family to take the business, so you must marry someone with Escobar blood. Cash what I am saying is you must marry one of my daughters." I felt my chest tighten as he said those words, as much as I want this opportunity I had Mya, and she was my world.

"Ruiz, as good as this sounds and it sounds hella good, I have to decline. The love of my life is in the other room, that's who I am going to marry." Right as we was about to speak we heard glass break, I jumped up to go check on Mya, because if he planned on hurting her for me to marry one of his daughter they would both die.

“Mya, what’s wrong?” She was on the ground crying and shaking.

“Did you know?” I was confused as fuck on what she was talking about.

“Know what ma?” She looked up and I followed her eyes, I was staring at a picture of Mya, aside from the nose and eyes so I was assuming it was her mother. I helped her stand up and seconds later Ruiz walked in.

“Cash, my friend what’s going on in here?” Mya turned to apologize and he just stared at her. Neither of them said anything just staring at each other, until Ruiz spoke. “Oh Dios mío (Oh my god).” He went toward the couch and took a seat.

“How do you know my mother?” Mya asked defensively.

“Your mother, Ana has kids.” He said that more to himself than us. “I had no idea, I haven’t spoken to my sister in about 10 years, and our father disowned her after she married your father.” He was shaking his head at the thought. “I have been looking for my sister since our father passed, but I couldn’t find any information on her and I always come up with something, so I figured she just didn’t want to be found. How is my sister?”

Mya

I swallowed the lump in my throat and went to sit down by my uncle. “She died 8 years ago.” The look on his face was heart breaking; I mirrored the look I had when I first found her.

“How did she die?” I thought about lying but I didn’t, I was nervous because I never even told Markell about what really happened to my parents.”

"She died of a drug overdose, the coroner said it was a bad combo of drugs that killed her. I had never seen her use drugs or anything, so I believe it was the events of the day that made her do it." He had tears running down his face as we spoke.

"What of Michael?" He asked in his heavy accent, I shook my head thinking of my father.

"My father was killed earlier that day in a bank robbery, right in front of me." I continued to run down the events of my life to him, and he just held me as we cried together. I have spent many nights crying on my uncle shoulders on my dad's side, but to be held by someone my mom cared deeply for was everything in this moment.

"Mya, I am so sorry for everything you have gone through as a child, and everything your young eyes have witnessed. I promise you that from here on out you will want for nothing, I understand that Cash has you, but know that I have you and Colombia has you; you my darling niece are royalty." He looked toward Markell as he spoke to me saying, "You have Escobar blood running through your veins." Markell nodded as if they were having their own conversation and I truly didn't care, I was just happy I was meeting my mom's family.

"How long are you staying? I would very much love to get to know you, and share some videos we have of your mother around your age and younger if you'd like." I looked at Markell and he nodded.

"I don't know how long we're staying, but I would like that." As he stood to walk away he looked at me and smiled, and I smiled back.

I let myself out of the house and walked around the estate, I heard shooting so my nosey ass went towards the sound and I saw a very handsome man shooting targets. I watched him and I guess he felt my presence, so he turned around and I be damned if I didn't cream my fucking bikini bottoms, he looked like Wilmer Valderama, the all grown up version. He walked toward me with cocky ass smile on his face, that said yeah I know I look good.

"Hola pretty lady, are you lost?"

"No, I am here visiting with my boyfriend." He nodded.

"You were looking pretty hard, you see something you like?" I laughed at his forwardness before replying.

"Yes, your gun, can I join you?" He led the way and gave me a gun and we begin shooting at moving targets, this was the most fun I have had in a year and I planned to enjoy it.

"Pretty good, you want to run through some techniques to improve accuracy?" I nodded happily and we went at it for hours.

Markell

"This changes everything Cash, you are dating my niece an Escobar, if you two wed then I will still honor the deal, but you must agree to visit Colombia at least once every three months for a year with Mya." I mulled over what he was saying and it wasn't bad, but I didn't want to rush Mya into anything.

"I love Mya Ruiz, she is truly one of a kind and made for my lifestyle, but I don't want to rush her into a wedding, especially not for power. He nodded and told me he understood, we talked for a while about Mya and he told me he wanted me to find out what happened to her father, so he could kill the bastard that unknowingly played a part in the death of his sister. I agreed to help him, because helping him helped Mya.

We went looking for Mya and I saw red, as I saw her having target practice with the one Colombian nigga I hated, Marco. They looked friendly as fuck and he was teaching her accuracy, the sad part is I have taken her to the range multiple times, and she never really showed any interest.

"Looks like my niece is a natural, the Escobar blood in her is showing." I could hear how proud he was, hell I was proud to but it doesn't change the fact that they were looking to friendly out there.

"Yeah, well I don't want her looking natural with no nigga but me." He laughed, but I was so got damn serious. I started walking over to where they were, I could just hear them laughing with each other, and making plans to get with each other again before she left; for him to show her some skills in combat.

"Over my dead ass body, and since I'm still breathing I guess that ain't happening." Mya turned around looking at me like I was pissing her ass off.

"Mya, you didn't tell me your boyfriend was Cash." He said with a smirk to piss me off.

"Yes, I am with Cash." She said with a smile and grabbed my waist. "Thanks for the training Marco, I really enjoyed myself, I'll see you at soon." We walked away, as I mugged the fuck out of him. It was no secret to anybody that Marco wanted to take over, but Ruiz only saw fit to keep him as a guard for whatever reason.

"Markell, slow down, you're walking too damn fast." Mya complained, in all fairness I was pissed as fuck she was smiling in another nigga face, but knew Mya would never betray me so I was just tripping.

"My bad ma, come here." I kissed her and she jumped up in my arms.

“Damn babe, you getting heavy.” I said jokingly and she smacked my ass upside the head.

“Shut up Markell, that’s not funny.” I kissed her again as my phone rang, seeing it was Mac I answered.

“What’s up bro?”

“Aye we need you back in Cali ASAP.” He sounded angry as fuck.

“What’s going on?”

“Somebody set your condo on fire; also two of our traps got hit.” I put Mya down so I could rub my fucking temples.

“Fuck man! I’ll be on my way in a few hours, if not I’ll leave tomorrow. Call a meeting for first thing tomorrow morning, I know this got James written all over it, so you need to make sure Jay punk ass is there, fuck bro. Let me finish handling shit out here and I’ll see you soon.” I ran everything down to Mya and I swear I saw fire in her eyes, we went back inside to talk to Ruiz, and our trip had just come to an end.

Markell

Landing in Los Angeles was bittersweet, a nigga was happy as fuck to be back home but pissed that niggas not only set my house on fire, but hit two of my valuable traps.

I was going to meet up with Mac, and I didn’t have time to drop Mya off, so her want to be a thug ass was riding with me. When we pulled up to the warehouse I wished I would’ve made her fucking change but there wasn’t any time, so my niggas was about to be looking all at my bitch.

She was wearing a sheer dress with a bikini top and some shorts, because that was all she had packed for our vacation. When we walked inside I could feel the eyes on Mya, I grabbed her hand so niggas would know that's me, and I don't tolerate no disrespectful shit.

"What's up bro, what up sis?" Mac said as we walked inside.

"What's up bro?" I said as we dapped up, Mya hit him with a head nod, since the day he grabbed her, she didn't fuck with him in any form.

"Getting down to business, does anyone want to tell me how the fuck two traps get hit in one day, and none of you niggas are dead? The fuck you do give them the drugs?" I waited and no one spoke. "So none of you niggas is going to speak up?" I reached behind me, and pulled out my gun ready to shoot all of these incompetent muthafuckas.

"No disrespect boss, but I don't feel comfortable talking business in front of bitches." Before I could shoot his ass Mya popped the nigga right between the eyes. Damn!

"Does anyone else have a problem talking business with me in here?" She asked and everyone said no. Damn, I couldn't wait to get her ass home. This young nigga I had put in charge of the house on Jefferson spoke up first.

"With all due respect Cash, My house was almost robbed but we handled that shit, it was four niggas, but they knew everything about the house, I'm talking about where the drop box was which floorboard had the money under it. You feel what I'm saying. My nigga Troy got hit but he gone be good, and Bear got a flesh wound but we handled our shit. You just got to hear what I'm saying." I heard what he was saying loud and clear, there was only three muthafuckas who knew the layouts to all the houses, which was Mac, myself and Jay.

"I want that nigga Jay now! Whoever brings me any information on where that fuck nigga is gets a bonus. I don't give a fuck how you get it, just fucking get it." I grabbed Mya hand and we walked the fuck out.

Mya got on the phone with her realtor to find us a new crib, while I rolled up a blunt, my mind was racing with all kind of thoughts and a nigga needed this. "Babe, he said we can meet him at the first property in about 25 minutes if you want to head over now."

"Cool babe, let's head over." We headed toward Malibu where the first place was and scoped it out, the neighborhood was quiet as fuck, which was to be expected, it was a cool little one story house with a circular driveway which was a plus, a nigga been wanting one of those for years.

"Cash, I don't want to see the inside, I already don't like it. It's the smallest house on the block." As I looked around she was right, it was the smallest house and they put the shit in between two big ass houses. Once the realtor pulled up we told his ass we needed something bigger, or something that isn't the smallest house on the block.

Mya

We drove about fifteen minutes up toward Pacific Palisades, and the houses over here were huge. The only specific thing I had in mind was being able to see the beach, as long as I could see the beach we were golden.

The house we pulled up to was a mini mansion and it was beautiful, it was made out of grey stone and had a black gate around it; it was beautiful as fuck but felt like too much. "Babe, this is beautiful but it feels like it's too much for us."

"Nah baby, this is perfect for a king and a queen, and that's exactly what we are baby. Royalty.

We continued to walk towards the front door, as the realtor told us about the property. It has 7 bedrooms with 2 of them being masters, 5 bathrooms with two offices, a living room and a den. The kitchen came with a brand new refrigerator that had the built in tablet. It had a massive backyard and sundeck. When I got to the first master bedroom I fell in love, from the patio you could see the lights from the Santa Monica Pier with miles of ocean behind it.

"We'll take it." I yelled out as they both looked at me, Markell with a smirk and the realtor in shock.

"Ms. Draught, I'm pleased to hear it, this property is 3.5 million dollars and comes with all the furniture inside, everything is brand new. You two would be the first owners since the property was just built from the ground up in February of this year." I loved the fact that no one had been here even more.

"Perfect, email us over the documents and we'll have everything to you this afternoon, also I'll have your check delivered via courier, but I need the keys now." He looked skeptical but handed over the keys, by the end of the night this would be our home.

Markell dropped me off at my old apartment in Santa Monica, while he went out to handle business, I was dying of boredom so I called up Naya, it had been months since we kicked but we always texted here and there.

“Damn bitch hell must be freezing over for you to be calling little ole me.” She said sarcastically.

“Hey bitch, how are you?”

“Bitch, bored as fuck, I was just thinking about going to the Carbon tonight, or a hookah lounge with my boring ass, we getting old bitch.”

“Bitch, speak for yourself I’m in my prime babygirl.” We both laughed as I continued, “But I don’t have any plans for the night so I could roll with you, if you’d like some company.”

“Hell yes bitch, pre-game at your place or mines?” I thought about it and told her to come here, I didn’t feel like driving to her place.

“Cool, let me get ready and I’ll be there in an hour.” We said our goodbyes and hung up, damn it felt good to be going out with my best bitch, and Lord knows I needed to let my hair down.

Naya

Finally a real bitch gets to speak; I have always been Mya’s flunky or the tag along. Life was simple for Mya, even without her parents she was still winning in life. I couldn’t stand her ass. I had been dating Jay on and off for almost 2 years and he had no fucking back bone, he didn’t want to move up in the ranks, he was cool with the little ass house he was over, but I wasn’t.

I wanted to be a boss’s bitch, I felt I needed to be kept, I worked a shitty ass job and lived in a shitty ass apartment, I didn’t even have central air in this raggedy muthafucka. So when Jay’s brother James, got out of prison and Jay confronted him on robbing the houses, the little wheels in my head starting turning.

I had convinced James to kill Jay, to take his place as being over the house and he could continue to rob him from the inside for a while with no one knowing what was really going on. Once the money started rolling in, Jay did shit I didn't expect.

He moved me out of my little raggedy apartment and bought us a nice ass condo out in Venice, not too far from the boardwalk.

Hell I was really feeling James, that was until he told me all of the plan and who else was a part of it. Now I don't know if the nigga was being greedy or if he just didn't give a fuck, but he was the a nigga I needed to be fucking with.

As I started getting ready for the club with Mya, someone knocked on my door. Getting up to go open it I saw the man of my fucking dreams standing there.

"What's up Naya is Jay here?" I rolled my eyes because he knew damn well Jay ass wasn't here, hell being honest we didn't even know if that nigga was dead or alive.

"Nigga, we both know Jay ain't here, but James is out running errands. Call his ass I need to finish getting ready." I walked away with some extra bounce in my hips.

"Where the fuck do you think you going?" I turned around and looked him in his eyes.

"I'm going to the club, with Mya." He had a devilish smirk on his face, like he was happy to hear that.

"Good I'll be with Cash, I'm going to try and find out where they moved to, but if for whatever reason I can't you need to try and get her to tell you." I nodded and he turned to walk away.

“Bye Mac.” I said seductively as he was leaving, and his big headed ass threw me a head nod. I didn’t care because I knew after tonight I would have his ass, one way or another.

I finished getting dressed and was on my way out the door, to meet Mya at her old apartment.

Markell

Sitting in my truck in front of the warehouse my mind was in overdrive, a nigga ain’t never had no issues and I really fucked with Jay, that was my nigga for years so I couldn’t think of a reason for his ass to fuck me over.

I got out and walked up to one of my traps over in Baldwin Hills, where my nigga Dre ran shit tight as fuck. Besides Mac, he was the only nigga I fucked with and that Mya felt was genuine, so I decided to pick his brain for a minute. As I walked from the car to the house I got all kind of love from the hood, whether a head nod or a what’s up that shit felt good, hell I gave back to the communities we were in so I felt the love.

“What’s up Cash, what brings you to my side of town?” He said as we slapped hands and brought it in with a hug.

“Shit, I just came to pick your brain about this shit that’s going on with these fucking snakes we got lurking around.” He nodded.

“I don’t think you want that boss, I like my life and I don’t want that shit to end for giving you my opinion, feel me.” We both laughed but he continued, “To be real, I feel like to many niggas know your layout, you need to tighten ship. Until you catch that nigga Jay, the only person who should collect and deal with the money is you, the only person who should know codes and shit is you, or Mya if you trust her like that. I'm not saying you can't trust Mac, but if you keep your eyes and ears to the streets you hear shit is all I'm saying."

I thought about what he was saying and I didn't want to look at my brother any kind of way, that was nigga 100 grand, I know if anybody had my back he did. Right?"

"Damn youngin, you really just laid it all out there no sugar coating or anything, that's what I asked for though, but let me get up out of here and change some shit up, I'll hit you up, I'm thinking I might need you to keep an eye on Mya for me for a while, I can't leave my queen out here unprotected."

"Hell nah, her mean ass need to protect me shit, bodying niggas in meetings like she trying to be a real life Grizelda Blanco." I laughed hard as fuck because he didn't know how true that shit was. I headed back to my car and texted Mya.

Me: What you doing baby?

Queen B: Getting ready to go out to the club with Naya.

Me: Were you going to tell me you were going to the club?

Queen B: I left you a note on top of your dinner babe.

Me: What club? What time you coming back?

Queen B: Carbon, I'll back by 11:30 babe, not late. I love you

Me: I love you too be safe.

I headed to the house to chill and wait for Mya; I hope she came home drunk because I was about fuck her life up tonight. I stopped Mya from hanging out with Naya on the sly because I didn't trust the bitch, she would eye fuck a nigga every time she came around. I hope her stupid ass went home tonight if not she was about to be a jealous bitch for real.

Mya

"Girl slow your ass down, I want to make it to the club in one piece." I yelled at Naya ass, she was going 120 down Venice Blvd. like she owned the fucking streets.

"Chill bitch, and live a little damn, I got this." She was looking at me and not the damn road as she drove; at this point I was ready to go the fuck back home.

"Look just slow the fuck down Naya damn." I yelled and she began to reduce her speed, I was overly annoyed and regretting coming out with her, I could have been at home sitting on my man's dick, instead I'm here with her worrisome ass.

We finally pulled up to the club and it was crowded as fuck, so I was just ready to find a small little couch to sit my ass down, I don't even know why I came out tonight, mainly I just missed my friend, and I didn't want to be up under Markell all the time.

"So Mya, how's married life?" I rolled my eyes at her dumb ass.

"Bitch, you know we not married."

"I'm just saying, you gave up your whole life for the nigga, you don't work anymore or hang out, I was just hoping you got a ring out of it." I was ready to slap her ass.

"First off don't speak on shit you don't know, that's what gets bitches killed out here." I stated in a serious tone. Her eyes bucked at my statement, she tried to play it off and recover though.

"So where did you guys move to, have you got a new place yet?" When she asked that all type of red flags went off, because no one knew that we were looking to move aside from Mac, everyone knew I still had my place so us moving or buying a place shouldn't even have been a thought in anyone's mind.

"We're just staying at my place for a minute, no rush you know." She nodded as if she was listening, but she was to busy texting away on her phone. I went to the bar and got me water, but pretended to be drinking Vodka, I wanted her ass drunk as fuck and those lips loose as fuck.

"Yeah girl but make that nigga cash out, bitch he swimming in cash, word on the street though is somebody in his camp gunning for his ass, so you would want to milk that cow why you can. I looked at her suspiciously and knew she knew more, this bitch was throwing more shade than a California palm tree.

As we danced on the dancefloor my mind was in over drive, thinking if my cousin was in on this shit. I mean, yeah my bitch was always wild and has fucked over plenty people I just knew I was the exception though. I tried to shake my thoughts as my song blasted through the speakers. I swayed my hips and thought of Markell.

You are unforgettable

I wanna get you alone

Now you wanna chose

Just popped bubbly in the 'cuzi

It's not good enough for me, since I been with you

I'm gonna sip on this drink, when I'm fucked up

I should know how to pick up

I'm gonna catch the rhythm while she push up against me

Ooh, and she tipsy

All I wanted to do was go sit on my husband to be dick, but I didn't drive and I be damned if this trifling bitch was about to fuck my life up.

I was sitting at the bar looking ridiculous sipping on my water like it was tequila or some shit, I even had his ass put a fucking stack of limes by me for effect.

"You know your pretty ass needs to be at home laid up somewhere right?" I turned my head quick as fuck.

"Dre! What are you doing here?" I started looking around for Markell.

"Chill sis he ain't here, he just told me to keep an eye on you with your little mean ass, why the fuck you sitting over here drinking water?" We both busted out laughing.

"Damn, just call me out, but nah I was peeping shit out and I needed a sober mind, but I'm glad you're here, did you come alone?" He looked confused as fuck by my question.

"Yeah, I don't stay to far, what's up boss lady." He put emphasis on boss like reminding me he wouldn't cross the line with me, and even though that's not what I meant, I could respect it.

"Nigga, not like that, pull to the front and I'll be right there." He nodded and I went to find Naya. "Hey Naya, I called us an Uber since we both fucked up, he should be out front now let's go." She nodded and we were out the door.

Once we got to the front of the club I saw Dre's black Yukon and we both hopped in, Naya was so busy texting that her bum ass never saw me grab a crowbar from the back. I wacked her across the head with it and Dre swerved a little. "What the fuck Mya? Don't kill that bitch in my car, and ain't that your damn cousin." I was unfazed about the fact that she was my cousin, hell she was my best fuckin friend, but loyalty is loyalty.

"I'm not going to kill her Dre damn, you sound soft as hell right now." I laughed at his ass because he was really bothered by what I just did.

"I'm not soft, but damn warn a nigga next time." He shook his head as I grabbed Naya phone to go through. "I see why you and Cash ass go so perfectly together." I smiled thinking about Cash, and then continued looking through the phone. The more I scrolled the more I saw red, I wanted to shoot her ass right here, but I couldn't just yet.

Markell

It was going on 4 o'clock in the morning and I had yet to hear from Mya's ass, I knew she was safe because Dre ass told me that much, but wasn't saying shit else. I got up to get dressed and turned on the iPhone find a phone feature and just knew she wasn't where I thought she was, my fucking phone must have been having a glitch.

I hopped in my car and sped all the way to Dre's duck off spot ready to kill both of their asses, if they were in this bitch doing what I'm thinking they doing. It usually takes me 20 minutes to get there, but I got to this bitch in 12. I grabbed my gun and cocked it as I walked toward the door.

I couldn't hear shit as I walked in and I looked all around that bitch, I walked down to the basement and what I saw had me even more pissed off. Mya was standing over a battered Naya with a gun in her hand.

"So you were in on setting my nigga up? All those questions you asked me tonight was to set my ass up to." Whack! She went across her face with the gun. I knew I shouldn't be but, I was getting turned on as fuck.

Naya whimpered as she tried to speak, but it was slightly muffled. "Speak up bitch, I can't hear your trifling ass." Mya said as she hit her again.

"It was all James idea, he knew they told Jay to kill him so he got to him before he could kill him, then he took over as Jay and been working with Cash ever since." She coughed as I thought about what she was saying, damn. "But Jay isn't dead, I know that much because he disappears with food for a few hours at a time every other day."

I knew I needed to find my nigga; damn I had really been slipping. I felt it was time to make my presence known so I walked in and Mya pointed her gun at me, I smirked at her. "Chill little killa it's just me." As she looked in my eyes, gone was the woman who was beating Naya's ass and back was my innocent baby girl.

"Markell, what are you doing here?" She asked as she kissed me.

"I saw you didn't come home and it was way past the club closing, I had to make sure you wasn't out on no hoe shit." She smacked the fuck out of me."

"Fuck you Markell, that's why you ain't getting no pussy nigga." I laughed at her because I was about to be all up in that shit like I lived there.

"I'm writing my name in that shit tonight ma." I smacked her on the ass when I put her down.

"Stop Markell, let me finish this. It's someone else that's working with them and I want to find out who it is, so we can go back to our regular life." I reluctantly let her go since she had a point.

I walked over to Naya and kneeled down before her, "Naya, if I promise to protect you from Mya, will you tell me who else is working with you and James?" The look on her face was one of uncertainty, she was weighing her options on if I could keep her safe or not. "I'm a man of my word, even if it means going against my woman, I'll make sure you're straight. Help me solve my problem and you'll want for nothing."

She coughed up a little bit of blood, and I leaned close to her lips to hear her better. "Mac, it's been Mac helping us." I stood up and walked away from her, I knew her ass was lying not my blood, my brother would never do this to me, and we built this together. I raised my gun and sent two to her dome. I said I would protect her from Mya, I never mentioned me.

"Babe, let's go." She followed me out to the car, and I waited for the cleanup crew to arrive before pulling out. I needed to keep a close fucking eye on my brother from now on.

Mya

After everything that went down with Naya, and Markell finding out about his brother, we decided to just head over to the new house since nobody knew where it was. I loved my new place but it wasn't home yet, so I was out running up a check on furniture and a few around the house accessories.

I finished all my shopping and decided to pay momma Ruth a visit. "No, I said I don't want these damn pills."

"Well your old ass about to take them, now sit down before I gel your ass." I took out my phone and started recording the abuse that was going on in my mother in laws room, they went back and forth with each other up until I saw the nurse raise her hand like she was about to hit Ruth.

"Bitch, I wish your rainbow wearing ass would hit my muthafuckin mother." I said as I opened the door, she looked spook as fuck which she rightfully should have been, all I know is she was about to end up with Marshall, and I was going to put her there.

"Mya, it's not what it looks like, she just wouldn't take her medicine."

"Bitch, I don't give a fuck, I'm taking my momma out of here and I recorded everything, so I will be pressing charges. Or I will be given a full refund for the full year she been here, since this might not have been the first time." She scurried past me and I pushed her ass down.

"Come on momma, I'll take you home with us after I talk to management." While she got herself together I went and played the video for the director, he agreed to pay us back for her full stay.

Once we left there I headed to hire an agency to care for her personally 24 hours a day, just in the privacy of our home.

"Thank you Mya, I don't want to be a bother on you and my son." I hugged her and we went out on a girl's day.

***

Once I got momma Ruth settled, she was out like a light. Her private nurse was going to arrive any minute, so I went and jumped in the shower to wash the day's events off of me and relax for a minute, five minutes after my shower the doorbell was ringing.

I threw on my robe and headed downstairs, I was shocked to find Markell cursing the nurse out, mentally kicking my ass for not calling him again I continued on toward the front door. "Mya, who the fuck is this and what is she doing here?" The look he had on his face was a mean ass mug, and any other time I would have laughed but due to everything that went on today I chilled.

"Give me a minute to get her settled, and I'll be back down to explain everything babe I promise." I kissed him on the lips quickly and showed the nurse to her room, which was next to momma Ruth's before going to find Markell.

"Why the fuck is there a stranger in my house Mya? With everything that's going on in the streets you thought this was a good idea?" He ran his hand down his face in annoyance, and I rolled my eyes in irritation due to him going off without letting me speak.

"You have a lot on your plate so I'll let that my house comment go for now, now as far as the stranger in our house, I went to see your mother today and I didn't like what I saw, so I brought her home and hired a private nurse to handle her care."

"What you mean you didn't like what you saw, what was going on with my mom's Mya?" I didn't want to tell him, so I went and grabbed my phone to show him the video instead. I watched his face go from normal, to upset, then to angry with some sadness in there. Due to everything that has been going on, he hasn't had the time to see her.

"Damn ma, I really dropped the ball. Fuck man, which room is she in Mya?" I told him and he ran to her room, if I wasn't sure before than I am now, that bitch has to go. Not only did she hurt my mom but she hurt Markell, in the year we been together I had never seen him dropped a tear, but as he stood over his mom he let them fall freely.

I slipped out of the room and ran upstairs, I through on my kick a bitch ass gear, some tights, black hoodie, and timberlands. I rushed out the house hoping to be gone and back before Markell even noticed I was gone, I pulled up the address that I swiped from the director's desk earlier for the nurse, and put in my GPS while riding to pull up by Cardi B.

Yeah

Bronx bitch till the day I die

I did my dirt and I ain't gotta lie

You can talk crazy on IG

But when I run up let them hands fly

I don't fuck around with no fucking clowns

Any niggas with me they fucking hounds

Any bitches with me they fucking down

So if you really bout it then pull up now

You stunk bitch

I know it sucks bitch

Yeah

Pull up bitch

Yeah

Like what's up bitch

When I pulled up on her block I cut the lights and rolled down her block slowly. As I approached her house, I saw more than one car in the driveway and it looked real familiar, a black on black Range Rover with custom words on the side. I took my phone out and took a couple of pictures. I threw my car in drive and rode off, I was pissed that I couldn't kill this bitch, but coming here I learned so much more.

Markell

Man everybody in my life was trying to give a nigga a heart attack, after checking on my moms and speaking to her nurse it made me grateful as fuck I had Mya in my life. I even slapped myself for not thinking about this before, I was about to go find her but being in this big ass house I decided to call her ass instead.

"Yes my love?" I heard wind in the background, so I knew she wasn't here.

"Where your black ass go Mya?"

"I'm pulling in to the garage now." I hung up on her ass and headed toward the garage, I didn't put my hands on women but at the moment, I wanted to fuck her little ass up.

"Where were you?" I no longer needed her to answer that question as I took in what she was wearing, her little sneaky ass was dressed in all black from head to toe. I just shook my head at her ass, and I had a real life gangster bitch in my life, who knew when and where to act like a lady.

"I went to see the nurse who called herself trying to come for my momma." She pouted as she spoke. I loved how hard she went for my mom, but I didn't want anything to happen to her either.

"Why didn't you tell me, we could have rolled out together ma, that's what I'm here for." I wasn't mad at her for wanting to do it, it just bothered me that she does shit without me.

"Well, when I got there I couldn't do it, there was a car there that looked familiar as fuck." She started going through her phone and pulled up a picture, when I saw that black on black

Range Rover I flipped out and threw her fucking phone. I was having an internal battle like I knew this shit couldn't be real.

My brother was with the nurse that was hitting my mom, I knew Naya said he wanted my spot but damn. Now I knew for sure Mac was gunning for me along with James, Jay was nowhere to be found and they had a nurse abusing my mom.

I pulled my phone out and called an emergency meeting, because I needed these niggas found ASAP, no more fucking around. I headed upstairs to get dressed, then hopped in my car and looked to my right at Mya.

"Babe, what the fuck is you doing?" I asked as I saw her getting her trigger happy ass in my car.

"I'm riding with you; mom's is straight so let's go. Every minute we sit here is a minute longer that we have a snake on our team, and I'm not getting out the car so let's go."

Once she said that we were out, Mya didn't even know what she was signing up for but I hope her ass was ready.

When we arrived at the warehouse no one was there but Dre, we slapped hands and stood off to the side while Mya went toward the office. "Where is everybody at?" Dre asked.

"Shit your guess is as good as mine, I sent you the same message I sent them niggas. I shook my head trying to figure out what the fuck is going on.

The door opened causing me and Dre to look up, and in walks muthafuckin Mac and James, along with a few of their flunkies and some of my team.

"Mac, what's going on bruh?" He looked high as fuck, red eyes and I could hear him sniffle every other second.

"What's going on huh?" He chuckled like my question was funny. "Let's see, you've made me an errand boy in our organization. Why is it that I haven't met the connect Cash? Why don't I have a private jet, and fancy ass condos in Westwood? Where the fuck is my rider at, huh? You got some fucking nerve asking me that shit nigga, when you living my life." This nigga was tripping hard as fuck.

"The connect didn't want to meet with you because you started slacking off. He saw you as a reckless ass nigga, this shit right here shows not only that, but you don't have no kind of loyalty." I don't know what they thought was about to happen, but I wasn't about to bitch up for no nigga, if a nigga was about to die I was about to talk cash money shit.

"My money started this shit, I went out and robbed that fucking bank not you, my young ass caught that body not you, I had nightmares every night, then got up and hugged the block every day nigga. Where was your ass at huh, oh yeah fucking school."

"What bank?" Mya said coming out with two guns raised, one pointing at Mac and one at James.

"So you was the little bitch crying over her dying daddy, I knew you looked familiar, my condolences little mama." Mac said with a sinister laugh.

I saw Mya finger itching to pull the trigger, and I be damned if my girl got shot because of Markell's snake ass. "You killed my father?" Mya asked in a shaky childlike voice, while Mac just smiled.

"Say it Mac, say it." Mac yelled, I could see the tears in her eyes but they wouldn't fall. She looked broken, and I just wanted to hold her but present circumstances wouldn't aloe that shit.

"James where is Jay?" I asked trying to take control back. He whispered to one of his flunkies and he walked out the door, next thing I know their dragging an unconscious Jay inside the warehouse. I shook my head because he and I both were being fucked by our blood brothers.

"So what now Mac, you're here waving guns, and I'm not going down like a bitch. I refuse to just hand shit over, so what's the deal?

"I want your connect, your bitch, then your life my nigga." He said as he winked at Mya.

"Well, that's not going to happen fuck boy." Mya said and smirked.

"Enough talking." James said, and pulled the trigger on Dre shooting him in the shoulder. I pulled out my gun and popped James ass twice between his fucking eyes. I looked to my left and Mya was taking out the flunkies, which kind of turned a nigga on seeing her in action like this.

Mac was slowly itching toward Mya so I popped his ass in his leg, when he went down I was still trying to get to Mya and then everything went black.

Mya

"Markell!" I yelled out, forgetting that we were in a shootout. I ran toward him making sure he was okay, when I got to him I saw blood coming from his head. I tried to apply pressure, but there was so much blood and I couldn't see where it was coming from. "Stay awake baby, please don't close your eyes, baby look at me." I cried into his chest as I sat there I felt something cold being pressed against my head, so I closed my eyes and heard two shots. When I opened my eyes Marco, and Dre had both killed the flunky who was trying to kill me.

I was confused on why Marco was there, until I looked around and saw my Uncle Ruiz's men all around the building killing everyone who was in there. We loaded Markell on an ambulance Marco had on standby, and then headed to Cedar Sinai.

I knew I looked a mess standing in this bourgeois ass hospital but right now but I didn't give a fuck, I needed my love to be okay.

"Mya! Mya!" I heard someone calling my name, I looked up and there was Dre, "Any word on Cash yet?" I shook my head and began pacing back and forth, I did this to keep from crying, so instead I thought about what the fuck just happened.

"For starters, what was left of Markell's team had to die, that nurse had to be dealt with, and Jay needed to get better as well. I shook my head at the fact that I was around my father's killer every day. We ate together, laughed together on countless occasions; I spent holidays with this man. Fuck! "Dre did anyone check to see if Mac was still there, or fucking dead? The look on his face was my answer.

"Man Mya, I was so caught on the flunkies and you that I wasn't even checking for Mac like that. I saw him and Cash going at it, so I figured Cash had got him because next thing I knew they both went down."

"I understand where you coming from, I'm just pissed off about it." Right when I sat down the doctor came out. "Family of Markell Castanendez."

"Right here, I'm his wife." I could tell by the look on his face it was bad news.

"Well Markell suffered a gunshot wound to the head, we were able to remove the bullet however, a part of his brain suffered an injury placing him in a coma, and we are unsure when he will wake up."

I felt my world stop, I fell to the floor and let out a gut wrenching scream. If I had to hurt then so was everyone else, they wanted a boss well now they got one.

Mya

6 Months Later

"Mya, let me help you out, you big pregnant and still trying to kill niggas. How would Cash feel about you trying to bust while you 8 months pregnant with his son, chill out that shit don't even sound right." Dre preached, but I was two niggas away from completely killing Markell's old crew.

In 6 months I had rebuilt his whole organization from the bottom up. New traps, new workers and now I was the only one who knew the location of the shipment and when it was arriving. I had successfully taken over, and with Dre and Jay's help it was running smoothly.

"I hear you Dre, but Cash isn't here, I need it to be safe for when my son arrives, plus Mac needs to be found and handled. I don't want him feeling as if he has allies all because we let a couple of niggas get away."

Dre ran his hand down his face in annoyance, but what I've learned is once I flashed my million dollar smile he just couldn't say no.

"Alright, but me and Jay will find these niggas and bring them to the spot, then you're crazy ass can kill them, deal?" I happily agreed with him before his petty ass changed his mind on helping me, and bringing me my midnight snack.

"Good, now hurry with my food I'm starving."

“Ole hungry ass, you always hungry ma but you good, I’m on my way and I been saving all these receipts for my lump sum refund when you drop that baby.” We both laughed before saying our goodbyes.

“Ms. Mya, I’m sorry to bother you but momma Ruth is having another one of her episodes.”

“I’ll be right there.” Lately momma Ruth had become violent with the more her disease progresses, she keeps asking for her sons, she couldn’t remember me because I wasn’t in her life that long, but being near my baby bump calmed her as if she could sense that it was a part of Markell.

I made my way downstairs toward her room, and could hear all kinds of yelling and shit being thrown.

“Bring me my son you damn she devil.” I tried to hold in my laugh, but the nurse was so scared she pissed herself.

“Momma Ruth, you have to calm down, your scaring Ms. Monica.”

“Fuck a Ms. Monica, her big back having ass is scaring me, ole gorilla looking ass.” I laughed so hard that Monica stomped her ass out the room. “Look at her shaking the whole damn house with those big ass feet.”

“Momma Ruth, you have to stop this, your scaring all the nurses.” I tried to be serious, but I was still laughing.

“Well good, take me to my sons.” Seeing that she was calm I backed out the room and made the call to send her to her son. “Hola! My beautiful niece.”

“Hola Uncle Ruiz, how’s everything?”

“Everything is perfectly fine and you? How’s my little nino baking?”

“Baking my last nerve, he is so active it’s crazy, he stays on my bladder all day.” I sighted as he let out a hearty laugh.

“It’s almost over, just make sure to send me pics and videos, I keep everything in cash’s room.” That brought a genuine smile to my face and tears to my eyes.

“Thank you! Do you think Ms. Ruth can stay there until after our little man gets here, she’s becoming more – he cut me off before I could finish.

“I’ll have the jet fueled in an hour, just have her ready to go, it’s time Marco comes home anyway.”

“Thank you so much. I’ll have her there.” We said our goodbyes and hung up the phone. Before I could relax there was a knock on the door.

“Hey Dre.” I said as we hugged.

“Hey bighead, You owe me a new future wife, running off all my girls with all their food runs,” he stated jokingly, “Or I could just ask Jay, or door dash or post mates or –

“Chill out, I’m joking girl.” I looked at Dre, and all of sudden I started to see him differently, he was handsome as hell. He stood at 6’1, pretty brown skin with tattoos covering both arms and the left side of his neck, he rocked deep waves in his head, and had the sexiest baby blue eyes.

“Mya, Earth to Mya!” I finally snapped out of my daze to him calling my name. “Huh, what you say?”

“I said you need to have a meeting with both me and Jay present at the table, to show just because you having a baby don’t mean niggas won’t get handled.” I nodded in understanding.

“Cool, I got to drop off momma Ruth, Let’s do that shit tonight with everyone.”

***

I dropped Ruth off and headed to our warehouse downtown, Not only was I about to make both Dre and Jay's presences felt, but I was about to shake shit up as well. I walked in feeling like I was a bad bitch, I had on some Fashion Nova jeans that my ass sitting right, with a black ivy park and some black timbs. I was dressed basic as fuck, but it worked for me. I took my seat at the head of the table with Dre to my right and Jay to my left; I could see the stares and questioning eyes because I usually sat alone.

"I'm going to make this short and sweet, I will be out of the country for a while and Dre will run things in my absence, if you can't reach Dre call Jay." I saw a few head nods and eye rolls but that was it. "Next some other shit will change, it's been quiet and I don't want niggas getting to comfortable, so you'll all get new burner phones. Leave the old ones on the table, all of you will be going to new traps, meaning you'll be working under new lieutenants."

"Man fuck this, you doing too much. I don't know why I'm working under a bitch anyway." I had two niggas posted outside so he wouldn't get far. "Anyone else want to leave now's the time." One other nigga got up and left. "Good, Dre it's all you."

Dre

It took a minute for a nigga to get a voice but I'm Drew Lambert, but everyone calls me Dre. I'm 24 years old and I'm an only child. I grew up cool, both parents had some good ass jobs. My mom was a teacher, my dad is a criminal defense attorney, and one of the best in California. My pops helped out a local dealer named King, and he would always drop jewels in my ear or money in my pockets, he and my pops grew close so I saw him a lot.

Growing up I wanted to be just like him now here I am. I met Cash through King, and been trapping ever since. I had no complaints working under Cash, aside from the fact that he didn't promote niggas. Niggas hardly ever moved up, which is how it was easy for shit to go down the way it did, but my loyalty ain't set up like that. Now Mya, put me in a position to make a name for myself on some real shit. She respected my decisions and didn't treat me like a peon.

"Alright, ya'll pick-ups will be handled the same way. Jay will be there on different days, same time frame. Watch the traffic that's at the houses, the house on piedmont keeps too much traffic and its drawing attention to us. Other than that we good, respect me and I'll respect you." Everyone nodded like they felt where I was coming from, and it made a nigga feel good ass shit.

"Also, before we go, you made a good choice by not leaving." Mya said, an in walks her Colombian killers dropping both bodies the floor.

"Everyone have a goodnight." Jay said, as Mya laughed walking toward the car.

"Baby girl you know you crazy right?" I asked her with one eye brow raised.

"You ain't seen shit yet?" She said as we loaded up in the car. I started the car and bumped Kevin Gates all the way to Mya's house.

"Thanks for everything Dre, I really appreciate you for being here for me." This the shit that was fucking with a nigga, mean ass Mya done opened up to me, had my ass feeling soft and protective ass fuck

"Anything for you Ma." Damn Dre why you say that shit.

"I'll hold you to that." She closed the door and walked off, damn Cash please wake up.

Mya

A month had gone by, Dre and Jay had business booming. The money was flowing nicely, I was able to kick my feet up and enjoy my pregnancy. Dre took care of the last few dudes who were lurking around, so the only issue left was Mac's rat ass.

As I thought about it I felt myself getting woke up, and my little nugget started moving. My phone rang, and as I looked at it I got overly happy that it was Dre. "Hellooo," I sung into the phone.

"What's up fat girl, what you doing?" I hated when he called me that, but loved it at the same time.

"Nothing, sitting here catching up on *Power*. Tommy is BAE!" He hated when I said that shit.

"Man bye Mya," I laughed at him.

"I'm joking, calm down what you doing?"

"About to pull up on you, I got real movies for us." I shook my head, every Sunday had become movie night for us.

"What movie?" I asked excitedly.

"It's a surprise, get the popcorn ready I'll be there in five!" I popped our popcorn and pulled out the gummy worms and shit, it legit looked like a kid sleepover. I saw the headlights hit the front window and knew he was here. I met him at the front door and hugged him.

"Hey Dre, what movie we watching?"

"Damn, I'm barely through the door little momma." He laughed and handed me the bag.

"Shottas!" I yelled out. This is my movie, Dre was the shit for hunting this down.

"Anything for your mad max looking ass."

"Don't ruin the moment, but that's my nigga though."

"He ain't even real though." Dre laughed heartedly, but I didn't give a fuck. Between Max and Tommy, lord I didn't know who I loved the most but they were my niggas.

We were watching the movie and saying our favorite parts, when a sharp pain hit me out of nowhere, "aaagh."

"Mya what's wrong baby girl?" "Dre, I think my water just broke." I cried hysterically, I was petrified. "Breathe ma. I'll run and get the bag. Meet me by the door just like you made me practice okay, can you do that?"

I nodded because I couldn't speak. Dre ran upstairs got the bag and came back down in record time. Once we were loaded up in the car, it took us 15 minutes to get to Kaiser. Dre went to get us a nurse and explained how far apart my contractions were, I was so grateful for him. The nurse got us settled in our private suite and brought me hella ice, with my hungry ass.

"Dre, thank you for being here for me, you've made it all bearable. My name rings bells thanks to you and Jay, but my midnight cravings and foot massages was all you. I'll never forget any of it."

I spoke from the heart as he sat and listened. He kissed me on my forehead and looked into my eyes and said, "There's no place I'd rather be." I was stuck in a trance as I looked into his beautiful eyes, and then I felt pressure. "Grrr aagh Dre, call the doctor he's coming Dre, I don't want to do this alone, how am I going to raise my son." I cried out, my emotions were overpowering the pain I was in.

"You will not do this alone ma, I will help you until Cash is awake, do you hear me?" I nodded at him as the doctor walked in.

"Okay Ms. Draught, let's see how far along you are, oh my I see the head, okay on the count of 3 I need a big push okay mom, lets go 1..2..3 push." I used all my strength and held on to Dre's hand as he coached me.

"One more time baby girl, one more push. Come on ma." I did as I was told, and was rewarded with the most adorable sound ever, my baby cries.

"Hey dad you want to cut the cord?" Dre looked at me and I nodded.

DRE

The feelings going through me were unexplainable as I cut the cord, the doctor cleaned him and placed him I my arms, a nigga cried real tears because Cash was missing all of this. Unbeknown to Mya, I had a camera set up in the corner so he could catch these moments when he woke up.

I walked over to Mya and handed her, her son, the look in her eyes was exhaustion and pure love. My little Mar'shawn Andrew Castanendez, he's so perfect Dre, god I wish he could be here." Mya said with tears running down her face.

"Don't do that ma, don't cry with sadness, celebrate your son." I watched her love on him until she fell asleep. I put the baby in the basinet they brought, and kicked my feet up in the chair. When I woke up I had several missed calls, so I hit Jay first.

"What's going on bro?"

“Man, I just got word from a friend that some of our old crew is selling work close by.” He said sounding stressed as fuck.

“They all gone, so you mean Mac’s ass?”

“Yeah bro, I’m about to go check it out, where you at?”

“I’m at the hospital, a prince was born my man.”

“No doubt, send my love. I’ll get with you later, let me check on little man.” I ended the call and sat back down. Damn, I couldn’t wait to have my own little rugrats someday.

“What you thinking about Drew?” Mya asked as she stretched her arms.

“Girl, don’t call me that white ass shit.” We laughed as little man started to cry. I picked him up and placed him in her arms carefully, and she popped out her pretty titty to feed him.

“Dre, if anything ever happened to me, you would be the person I know my son could count on; I guess I’m asking would you be his god father?”

“Hell yeah!” I jumped up out my chair, and hit the milly rock I was so happy.

“Boy sit your non-dancing ass down please.” We spent the remainder of the day shooting the shit and Mya and one of her nurses trying to teach me how to change a damn diaper, which was really feeling like fucking rocket science.

“Man fuck y’all, where the pull-ups at?”

Mya

6 weeks later

My life had quickly gotten into a routine, I was now coordinating from home as far as shipments went. I started looking into a business I could open, I knew I wasn't opening no damn salon, tattoo parlor or nail shop like every other drug dealer, I wanted something different.

I wanted something family oriented, like a day care or maybe even a rec center. Deciding to go with a rec center, I called up my realtor and told him to start looking for properties near a park. Next I call up my uncle and checked on Markell.

"Hola beautiful, to what do I owe the pleasure of this call?"

"Uncle Ruiz, I always call you, but I was calling to check on Markell." I was hoping that he gave me some good news for a change, a finger moved anything.

"No change my love, I will do everything in my power to bring him back to you, but it's not much I can do, how's my young bull?" I just smiled thinking about my boy.

"He's good, just getting chunkier by the day and stop sending him clothes he can't even fit, it's a waste of money." My uncle had sent hundreds of clothes ranging from newborn to 6T; I knew I wouldn't have to worry about clothes for a while.

"Nonsense, he is the only boy in our family so he is a king in the making." That thought never crossed my mind, my son would become the plug once he was of age, whether or not that's the path he wanted to take or not.

"You're right, well keep me posted and I'll call soon."

"Goodbye my niece and Dre is a great man, I know you love Cash as do I, but don't hide from the possibility of love, we don't know when or if he'll wake up." I let his words marinate as we hung up, and got ready to give Shawn his bath.

Dre

Sitting here counting this money, all I could think about was Mya and little man. I know he's not mine but cutting cord and holding him in my arms made me want to step up and be a better man, I wanted to be there for them both.

Cash and I weren't best friends or shit, but I had to respect his hustle, and couldn't see myself pushing up on his lady especially to get shot the fuck down. I rubbed my hand down my face, and decided to throw caution to the wind I sent her a message.

Me: What's up fatty, what you doing?

Boss Lady: Giving little man a bath, what you doing?

Me: Counting.

Boss Lady: Come through and I'll help you, then we can watch Boyz in the hood … Yo fave!

I banded up the money that I just counted, through everything in the bag and headed over to Mya's. When I got there the door was already open so I headed inside, I walked up the stairs and found them inside the nursery, where she was rocking him to sleep.

They both smelled of Johnson and Johnson. Her hair was wet and curly, bringing out the features of her beautiful face, she had on a floor length silk gown and a matching robe, but it wasn't tied so I could also see her erect nipples through the thin fabric, damn.

"Hey Dre, you got here quick. What'd you do run all the lights?"

"I might have blown through a stop sign or two." She giggled as she stood up to lay him down. Once he was in bed I just admired my godson, he made me ready for my own. "You ready for movie night?" I asked her trying to get my thoughts off planting my own son up in her.

"Yes sir, I already set it up, all we got to do is press play." We headed toward the living room to enjoy our night. I was even prepared for her to irritate the fuck out of me when Rickey gets shot.

***

I didn't remember pressing play or falling asleep, but as I woke up and looked down Mya was laying across my lap asleep. I got up and carried her to her room, as I turned to walk away she grabbed me, "Can you stay?" I nodded my head and was heading toward the couch when she spoke again and said, "In here."

I took off my shirt and shoes then laid down, she snuggled up in my arms and I held her as we drifted off to a peaceful sleep.

I woke up to the smell of bacon and pancakes, a nigga was hungry as fuck, so I went to the bathroom to handle my hygiene. After washing my face and brushing my teeth, I headed down stairs following the smell of the food.

Once I got to the kitchen I saw baby Shawn sitting in his bouncer, so I picked him and showed him some love for a few minutes before laying him back down. "Good morning sleepy head." Mya said as she strolled her ass in to the kitchen, she had the sexiest morning head I had seen on a chick.

"Good morning ma, what you got planned for the day?"

"Nothing really, just call and check on these places with my realtor and then probably just chill here with my little love bug, why what's up?"

"I got somewhere I want to take you, so get you and little man dressed by three o clock. I'll be here no later than three thirty to pick you guys up, make sure you guys dress comfortable." I kissed her on her cheek and ran out of there quick, before she became too difficult and started asking 101 questions.

Mya

I was irritated with Dre because it was already fucking twelve in the afternoon and he wanted me to be ready in three fucking hours? Dre knows I need more time for the baby alone, and his ass gave little details on where we were going.

I hurriedly cleaned up the kitchen from our breakfast, bathed Shawn and lotioned him down, then proceeded to dress him. Once he was dressed I put him down for a nap, so I could shower and get dressed.

I got my clothes and checked the time, it was two thirty and I was just now about to get in the shower, so I made it quick. When I hopped out the shower I started to moisturize my skin, but my baby started to cry, so I just threw my robe on and headed to his room.

As I got closer to Shawn's nursery I heard a man's voice that I knew didn't belong to Dre, I reached in a dresser drawer that was in the hallway and grabbed one of the any guns that we had stashed around the house, courtesy of Dre. I walked closer to my son's room and his crying increased coming around the corner, I cocked the gun and pointed it toward the man holding my baby, he turned around at the sound of my gun cocking. I gasped while still holding the gun at him.

"Put my fucking baby down Marco." He kissed Shawn's head and then laid him down and held his hands up in mock surrender. "How'd you get in my house?"

"Well, for a queen pin you have no security, and your windows are not locked. Your son is next in line for the throne, he will head not only the drug trade on the west coast and in Colombia, but he will be head of the Colombian Cartel. Many people will pay good money for him to die." I had no idea Ruiz was involved with the Cartel, let alone the head of it but I guess thinking now it makes sense.

"Including you Marco? You want my son dead?" I asked with my gun still trained on him.

"Mya, I have served your uncle for sixteen long years." I laughed cynically ready to shoot his ass right here if need be. "That's not an answer Marco, come with me, let's step out of my son's room." He began walking toward me, I was momentarily distracted by Shawn's crying that Marco used it to his advantage and got away. I could have went after him, but in that moment my son was more important.

I walked over to my son and picked him up, I held him while I cried into his little body. "I'm sorry for this life you have been born in to, but I will protect you my little love bug." I cried for my son, for his safety and his future. I heard the stairs creek and I held my baby tighter, and grabbed my gun back up off the floor and pointed it toward the doorway. "Mya, where you at?" I sighed in relief as I heard Dre's voice."

"Yo ma, why is the door wide – he stopped talking and looked at me. "Mya, why the fuck do you have a gun in your hand and holding little man, what's going on?"

"Marco happened. Let me through something on, so we can get the fuck out of this house with my baby." He grabbed Shawn and I ran to my room to get dressed, I didn't even feel like combing my hair, so a messy bun was what it was today.

Marco had just crossed a major line, they thought I went hard as a mourning girlfriend, but I was about to go ape shit crazy as a fucking mother whose only child is in danger.

Dre

I saw fucking red as Mya told me what happened, Marco had a lot of nerve to come up in here the way he did. He basically just declared war with Ruiz, by coming up here on some rah rah shit. I was also pissed that Mya never told me about her relationship to Ruiz, shit everyone knows you don't get emotionally involved with the plugs family.

"So, you never thought to tell me you were the connects niece, if I knew that I would have moved differently Mya, you should have been protected at all times." I was pissed off anything could have happened, me being next in charge that shit would have made me look bad as fuck, and I really don't know what the fuck is going on.

"I didn't think anything of it, I think Marco tapped my phone. My uncle Ruiz, and I just had a conversation about Shawn, being the only boy meaning he was next in line to –

"Take over the family business." I cut her off to finish her sentence. I took a deep breath to keep calm. "Just sit back, let's enjoy this day and we'll worry about everything else tomorrow." I looked in my rearview at Mar'Shawn and said a silent prayer, that no harm would come to him, and as long as I had breath in my body it wouldn't.

When we pulled up to our destination Mya's eyes grew big ass saucers. "Dre, where the hell are we."

I laughed "Calm done, my parents are having a BBQ and I wanted them to meet you, and little man now fix your face and let's go."

"Why am I meeting your family? Are you about to propose to me or something? If you are just not today please because I'm not cute enough." She said it jokingly, but only if she knew I would love to propose to her ass.

"If I asked would you say yes? I got out the car without waiting for her to reply, I wanted the thought to linger in her head for a minute. I grabbed Shawn's car seat and went around to open Mya's door. I grabbed her hand as we walked toward the door when suddenly Mya stopped.

Mya walked closer to me and kissed me, so quickly I almost wasn't sure if it had happened. She continued walking toward the door, I jogged up to her and pulled her closer then I gave her a nice long sensual kiss.

When we parted we just looked at each other, until I opened the door for us to walk inside. I walked in first and looked around because Mya was nervous as fuck and literally shaking, I followed the smell of the BBQ coming from the back yard and a nigga stomach started growling. Shit, I was hungry as fuck and wasn't ashamed to admit it. I yelled out for my mom's and pop's as we kept walking.

"Hey son, how are you doing?" My dad asked as we hugged.

"I been good pops, real good. This is Mya, and this little guy is Mar'Shawn but we call him Shawn." I said proudly.

"Hello Mya, it's nice to finally meet the woman my son can't seem to shut up about and I see why. You are a very beautiful young lady, and this little guy is going to be a heartbreaker for sure, may I hold him?" Mya nodded and my pops picked him up and walked off, I knew we wouldn't be holding him for hours.

Mya

Dre went around introducing me and Shawn to everyone and it felt good, I had never been introduced to anyone's family, they were all pretty sweet except for one guy who stood out. It wasn't that he was mean or nothing, he just kept fucking staring at me as if he knew me or had an issue with me. His name was King, he had an aura about him that screamed Boss and his mannerisms seemed familiar, but I shrugged it off and tried to enjoy the party. I had met everyone except Dre's mother, and I was starting to think the women wasn't going to make it to the BBQ. I watched Dre interact with his father and I loved their relationship, he would laugh and joke, and play hit each other every few minutes as if they were the best of friends. I loved it, I wanted that for my own son someday.

"Excuse me is this seat taken?" The man I who I knew as King asked.

"Depends on what you want it for?" I said with too much venom dripping from my voice, I tried to remember where we were, so I threw a quick smile on my face to hide the mug that was plastered, but my tolerance for bullshit these days were low as fuck.

"Whoa ma, I came in peace, my question is do you?" I gave him a look that could kill in that minute. "Let me finish, I have known Dre for a long time and never has he shown this much interest in someone, if you hurt him I will kill you. Queen Pin or not, the Colombians won't be able to save you." He got up and left after speaking his piece and I was ready to go.

I got up to go find Dre, he was doting on Shawn with his father and it was a beautiful sight. I walked over to them admiring the sight before me. Dre was slowly creeping into my heart on accident and I didn't want him to stop, he was just natural around me and me around him, I never made moves without speaking with him and vice versa.

I was walking toward them when a voice from behind me said "You must be Mya, I'm Dre's mother Rochelle, it's nice to meet you." I stuck my hand out for her to shake and she just hugged me instead.

Even though I was previously ready to go, I stayed to talk to his mom and boy was I glad I did. She gave me so many parenting tips and her general conversation was beautiful, Dre and his dad came over and joined us, the conversation lasted for at least two hours.

It was going on ten o'clock when we finally decided to leave and boy was I tired. I was out like a light the moment he started the car.

***

When I felt Dre tapping me I opened my eyes, and lord I was at the most beautiful house I had ever laid my eyes on. It was modest yet still beautiful. "Dre, whose house is this?"

"It's ours or it could be. I'm not counting cash out, but for almost a year I have been able to get to know you as a person, not just mean ass Mya, that the streets are familiar with, but the real you, and with Shawn these last 6 weeks shit just feels right. I want to try this out and see what could become of Mya and Dre."

I was in tears by the time he was done talking, I couldn't even speak so I nodded as he grabbed my face and kissed me. I'd be lying if I said it didn't feel right, my whole body was on fire and I wanted him in the worst way.

“Come on ma, let’s get little man inside.” He went and scooped Shawn out the car seat, and led the way in to our home.

Dre

11 months later

“Dada Dada Dada.” I smiled as Shawn ran around from room to room yelling that out, he began to call me that around 8 months, and Mya ass was jealous as fuck because she wanted him to say mama so damn bad, that she would walk around pouting for hours at a time. I laughed as I continued watch Mya chase Dre, he snatched his diaper off and was out of here.

“I’m glad you find this shit funny Dre, everyone will be here soon and he won’t be ready. This is his first party I want it to be perfect.” Mya, complained as she tried to chase Shawn’s naked ass around the house.

“Come here son; let’s go get dressed for mommy.” He ran into my arms yelling, “Dress for mommy.” The best way he could.

“See Dre, my own son thinks I’m a joke.” I laughed at her dramatic ass and took little man toward the bathroom for his bath. When I finished cleaning him up and getting him dressed his little ass laid down for a nap. I headed back toward the living room and Mya was on the phone with someone.

“No I can’t make it, it’s my son’s first birthday, alright I’ll be at the airstrip by one o’clock in the morning, make sure it’s fueled and ready to go, this shit better be important.” She said and ended the call.

“Who’s that babe?” I asked her, and I swear she jumped a little at the fact that I had caught her ass on the phone. “That was umm Ruiz, he was just calling to wish Shawn’s bad ass a happy birthday.” I nodded my head and decided to leave the situation alone, but just know that come tonight when she thought she was sneaking off on me her ass had a another thing coming.

Once Mya and I were dressed we went and woke up Shawn, so we could take our family photo. Mya had gotten me and her shirts that said Marshawn’s first birthday, with his picture on the front and mine had daddy on the back and hers said mommy.

My mom and dad also wore shirts that matched ours, just with grandma and grandpa on the back. A nigga was feeling good as fuck, the only thing that bothered me was the fact that Cash could wake up at any moment, and all this could be taken away from me. I would take on the world for my little family, but at the end of the day they were also Cash’s family.

Walking out to the backyard to check on things, I admired our home. I loved the set-up we had going on, the entire back yard had a tropical feel to it, Mya had rented some lady to come out and bring all Shawn’s favorite animals. We had pigs, horses and some more weird ass shit in our yard. It was a few of the kids from his day care here with their parents, and everything ran smooth as fuck.

“Okay everyone, it’s time to sing happy birthday.” My mother yelled from inside the house and she began walking out with the cake. “Where’s the birthday boy?” I laughed because my mom was quite a character and could be really animated at times.

I scooped Shawn up and carried him to the table for everyone to sing happy birthday, and he just put his hand all up in the cake. We knew wasn’t nobody about to allow they kids to eat that shit.

“It’s okay I brought a back-up cake just in case.” Mya yelled before running inside, she rolled a two tier elephant cake out from the house with sparkler candles on it, and all the kids went wild. I was in love with Mya at this moment more than before because she just looked in her element.

I was sitting back watching the kids play when my phone rang, looking at the screen I saw it was Jay. “Hey bruh where you at, you damn near missed the party.” I chuckled because he always wanted to be fashionably late.

“Man some shit just went down, get over to Piedmont house ASAP.” He spoke and then ended the call. I went up to the room to change in to something more street savvy, and was out in five minutes I knew Mya would be pissed but she would understand.

I made it to the trap on Piedmont in fifteen minutes and shit looked normal, so I was confused as fuck, I hopped out the truck and went to check shit out. I open the door and walked in and saw Jay standing there, “What’s going on bruh what’s the problem?” He looked at me with a heavy heart and shook his head.

“Our trap got hit but they didn’t find anything, they killed two of our men whom I’ve already gotten cleaned up and shit, the people who hit us didn’t find anything simply because they didn’t know where to fucking look.” He dragged his hand down his face and continued, “They checked our floorboards and shit but you know Mya decided not to fuck with floorboards.” I took in what he was saying.

“So you saying Mac hit our trap and thought we would have shit setup the way he had his shit setup, what the fuck kind of sense do that make?” I wasn’t really expecting an answer I just needed to hear myself say that dumb shit out loud.

“Mac wasn’t alone though bro, look at the tapes.” I took Jay’s phone from out his hand to look at the video, we had camera’s set up in all our traps, but only we could see the footage. The whole thing could be controlled from our phones, it couldn’t be traced nor hacked and if we were raided it would be deleted before they could even unplug the shit.

My heart sped up as I watched both Mac and Marco raid our shit, but Marco wasn’t really doing shit except making himself seen, he stared at the camera the whole time before walking off. “The fuck kind of shit is this nigga on?” I shook my head because I was in disbelief. I continued to watch the video, he wrote something down on a piece of paper, I squinted my eyes to try and see it but I couldn’t make it out.

“What the fuck he write Jay?” Jay reached in his pocket and handed me a piece of paper that read *“Enjoy your family while you can.”* I saw red and socked a big ass hole in the wall, stayed with Jay long enough to get some new niggas in the trap, and I took the money from out of there with me and headed home.

Looking at my phone I saw that it was eleven thirty at night, so I made it back in time to see what Mya excuse would be for leaving. I walked into the house and saw no one, everything was cleaned up and my parents were gone. I walked into our room and I noticed Mya was in there packing a bag. “Where are you going Mya?” She rolled her eyes at me and continued to pack. “Do you not hear me talking to you?” I grabbed her arm and turned her around, her face was wet with tears running down them. “What’s wrong ma, this ain’t us. We don’t keep secrets and have attitudes, now talk to me.” She looked everywhere but at me, and that shit had me worried as fuck.

"I'm heading to Colombia, Ruiz called me this morning and said it was important that I head there right away, but I had to wait until after Shawn's party because nothing is more important than that." I nodded in understanding and she continued. "He called me again to tell me that Marco was back in the states and was coming with a message for me." I rubbed her shoulders as she talked not wanting to say that he was already here so I just stood back and let her vent.

"I really don't want to do this anymore Dre, I just want to worry about taking care of my son and starting my business, who wants to marry and settle down with a fucking Queen Pin?" I grabbed her face and kissed her, I needed her to relax and I could feel the stress and tension leave her body; she jumped up and wrapped her legs around my body I held her with one hand and ripped her shirt with the other. "Too many clothes baby girl." She giggled and helped me take her shirt off, I sucked on her nipples and she moaned in my ear, I loved the way her moans sounded.

"Make love to me Drew." Her wish was my command; I kissed every part of her breast and laid her down on the bed while trailing kisses down her toned stomach. "I want to have your baby Drew." She moaned in my ear, that shit made a nigga smile hard as fuck.

"I thought I'd never hear those words ma." I whispered in her ear while biting on it, I pulled her pants down and began to feast on her pussy like it was the last meal I would ever get. I kissed her pussy as she came in my mouth, I slapped her on the thigh and told her to turn around, and all in the same motion I slipped inside of her and pounded in her pussy as hard as I could.

"Fuck Drew, shiiiiit I'm about to cum baby wait." She moaned loudly, I smacked her on the ass and continued my assault on her. "Shit ma, don't ever give my pussy away, tell me you won't." I pushed deeper inside her and she couldn't speak.

"It's yours baby, oh god it's your pussy, I promise I won't give it away." She was trying to run from me so I held her little ass in place.

"Nah ma, where you going? Huh, you trying to run from me already?" I picked my speed up and began to pound into her hard as fuck.

"Baby I'm cumming, oh god it's right there Dre." I blocked what she was saying out because my nut was right there and as I felt her release, I released right along with her and my body went limp, causing me to collapse on top of her.

"Get off of me with your heavy ass." She said through giggles I kissed her on her shoulder blade, then again on her lips then picked her up so we could shower.

Mya

I was on cloud nine as we showered each other, the way Dre fucked me just now I knew he loved me, it was rough and passionate. For the last eleven months life with him has been wonderful, and I couldn't imagine myself with anyone else.

I missed Markell dearly, but at this point I just wanted him to get better for Shawn, but I didn't see myself leaving Dre. He was caring, funny and ran the streets without running the streets. He kept his home happy and our workers happy, but above all of that he made my son happy.

I'd watched him on numerous nights put Shawn to sleep by telling him stories of a super hero named Markell, and he showed him pictures of him as well. Dre took the dad role seriously, but never tried to take away the possibility of Shawn knowing he had another daddy.

“What you over there thinking about with your big headed ass?” Dre asked as we got dressed for our flight to Colombia.

“I’m thinking about you, Dre I never thought we would be where we are now, but for almost two years you have been my rock. I can confide in you on a friend level, and you’ll give me that advice with no judgements or questions asked. I know that you love me because I can feel it, and see it every day.” I walked away from him and reached in to my night stand drawer, and pulled out a box I have been holding on to for weeks.

“Where is all this coming from ma?” He asked looking worried I laughed at him and walked back over to where he was, I kneeled down and grabbed his left hand I swallowed really hard and asked the question that has been burning in the back of my mind.

“Drew Cairo Lambert, will you marry me?” I closed my eyes as I waited for his response when one didn’t come. I opened my eyes and he was kneeled in front of me with a beautiful princess cut diamond ring, I laughed because we just got each other perfectly.

“Well Mya Draught, only if you’ll agree to marry a nigga like me?” I nodded my head as we laughed and we kissed each other so fucking long and deep, I’m sure we could have gotten another round in if it hadn’t been for the doorbell.

“You ready to see the beautiful country of Colombia?” I asked him.

“With you by my side, I’m ready for anything.” With that we held hands and walked toward our car.

***

Once we landed in Colombia things were different then how they were with Markell, there was no fancy hotel or long rides. I was flown directly to my uncle Ruiz's private air strip seven miles from his estate, he had this here just in case he needed a quick getaway, plus it made it easy to get work in and out of the country.

Our driver picked us up and drove the few miles up to the main house where Ruiz was waiting on me. We got out the car and damn if Dre wasn't looking good as fuck. I looked down at my hand and admired my ring, in a short time from now I would be Mrs. Mya Lambert. I was hyped as fuck and this damn meeting was killing it, I should be fucking the shit out of my soon to be husband, not meeting my uncle to discuss Marco and the fate of the cartel.

Once we reached the door, my uncle's maid Esmeralda answered, "Hello Mya, your uncle is awaiting you both in his office." She said before walking away.

I headed toward the office with Dre hot on my trail, the closer I got I could hear multiple voices; I looked at Dre as he looked at me, and I knew just as I knew the voice he did.

I knocked on his door and he said to come in, as I walked inside I felt as if my legs would give out at any moment. "Markell?"

Markell

"Markell?" I knew her smell before she even opened her mouth to speak. Standing in front of me was my future wife, the woman who made my life better and had given me my first son.

"Hey baby mama." I said to her and chuckled, she scrunched her face up at my choice of words.

"I am not, nor will I ever be a baby mama, that shit is so disrespectful." She was getting fired up and I missed that shit. I was about to tell her to calm down until I saw Dre put his hand on her back and without having to say a word she calmed down, her demeanor had just changed and I wasn't feeling that shit not one bit.

What's up Dre, how you been?" I asked him as we slapped hands.

"I been good, just living life and doing the family thing you feel me?" I didn't know whether to take that as a shot at a nigga or not, so I let him have that.

"Yeah, I feel you, shit I'm trying to get like you." I spoke and only if he knew how true those words were.

"I'm sure there's someone out there for you my man." He replied and before I could speak, Ruiz spoke up.

"Okay gentlemen, if you're done having your pissing contest we can start." He got up and kissed Mya on the cheek and they hugged, damn I miss feeling her body, kissing her soft ass lips and the moans she would make in my ear.

"Dre, I am glad you could make it, I hear nothing but good things from all of California as well as Nevada. I even see you've managed to now supply all of Arizona, that is no easy task my friend." Ruiz spoke to him and I was getting pissed, I had tried to break in to Arizona for years with no luck because they weren't fucking with niggas down there like that.

"Slight work Senor Ruiz." He replied, he wasn't boasting or rubbing shit in I was expecting something, but the nigga wasn't being shit but humble.

"Now down to what I have called you down for, about two years ago I told Markell that he could become me, I promised him my position, with a clause." I stared Mya down as he spoke to check out her reaction to what he was about to say. “Mya and Markell have to be married in order for this to work; now I understand that the situation has changed and you are now with Dre, but I am getting old and your son isn’t old enough to take over, and won’t be for quite some time.”

I watched as Mya eyes got watery and her skin was beginning to turn red, she looked at me with nothing but hatred, there’s was no longer any love, hell not even a hint of like.

“No.”

“What did you just say?” I asked Mya.

“I said no." She stood up and again Dre grabbed her and she calmed down, he whispered something on her ear, and she took a deep breath in and released it before taking her seat back.

“Mya, this has already been arranged, the other cartel families will not allow a woman to run this organization, they are expecting a wedding by the end of this year, and a wedding will be what they will get. They will not accept my daughters simply because they have no children and you already have a son.” I smirked as I looked over at Dre, but he looked unbothered.

“With all due respect Senor Ruiz, not even twelve hours ago I proposed to this woman right here and she said yes, I will not allow her to marry another man, especially if she does not want to. I understand you two have an agreement, but the way I see it is you can give the other families a wedding between Mya and myself or there will be no wedding.” Dre spoke and Mya set there with a smirk on her face, the smirk that said her panties were wet and he was getting some pussy, my pussy later on tonight.

“Let me think this over with the families and see what they say, you all do good work so this will be an easy sell, I’m sure if one of you were to handle Marco, that would help smooth over there decision, since he has been a pain in all our asses, but mine especially. I will let you know in three days' time." He stood up and we were all headed to have brunch before departing.

Mya

Pissed wouldn't even began to explain how I feel and neither would hurt, I had so many questions running through my mind, like how long have you been up? How can you be up and not think to call home?" My mind was in overtime, but Dre kept me grounded.

I was trying not to be a petty bitch or nosey but I needed answers. "So Markell, how long have you been up from your coma?" I literally took a sip of my tea as I asked him and waited on an answer.

"I have been up for almost four months, going on five." I could have shot his ass right where he sat; he answered it so nonchalantly that it was as if it was yesterday.

"Uncle Ruiz, I called you monthly for updates you never said anything." I sipped my tea again because this shit was unbelievable.

"He asked me not to tell you, I did however tell him you two share a son, so I don't know why he decided to not communicate with you, I apologize for not being honest with you." I smiled at my uncle because he was sincere in his apology, even though I was still pissed at him for arranging marriages and shit.

"So, you knew you had a son and still didn't bother to call, and at least ask for a picture or how he was doing? Wow Cash, you are a true piece of shit." I said as I continued my lunch.

“Baby it wasn’t that, a nigga just had a lot of thinking and recuperating to do, you just don’t understand ma.” I nodded my head because that was the first thing he said that I agreed with.

“I agree, anyway Dre and I are going to go explore Bogota before we return home, I’ll stop bye to say bye before I we depart.” I spoke to my uncle and kissed him on the cheek.

***

Dre and I enjoyed our trip so much that we decided to stay and spend the night here, I called his parents at least six times yesterday checking on Shawn, which after call four they stopped answering and now I was freaking out.

“Dre, can you just call and check on him please, your mom stopped answering my calls.” I pouted hoping that he would give in and call for me.

“No can do baby girl, you are not putting me in the middle of you and mom’s shit, now what you can do is help me find this Marco nigga so we can kill him, get married and run all of Colombia.” He said as he kissed me on the top of my head.

“You really think we can do this, run Colombia?” I don’t know why I asked, because he was so focused he could do anything.

“Hell yeah ma, we can do anything we put our minds to.” He kissed me on the top of my head and we started looking for Marco, with help from our Cali connects and Colombian workers we were hoping it would be easy.

Dre

I couldn't even lie and act like I wasn't pissed; they not only tried to take a niggas status, but my wife. When I walked in that room I just knew Mya, would run in jump in his arms or some shit like they do in those corny ass white people movies, but shorty never let my hand go nor left my side.

We'd spent two of the three days thinking and trying to come up with a way to find Marco, until it finally fucking hit me, if I find Mac I'll find Marco since their working together. "Babe, wake up." I nudged Mya ass, she had been sleeping all fucking day, and I needed her crazy ass Colombians to go sit on that nigga. I had every day niggas but a few people Mya had gotten from her uncle were able to blend in, one nigga went as far as to get up at six in the morning and cut this nigga grass just to kill him.

"What baby, it better be important I was about to get some good dick from Mad Max." She said as she sat up.

"What I tell you about that dream cheating shit, don't get homie fucked up." She laughed and went to brush her teeth.

"So what's up, why you stopping me from getting my beauty sleep?" I mushed her because she was always talking about some damn beauty sleep, like she wasn't the sexiest woman in my world.

"Alright, I need you to call Hector and Ricardo; I need them to find Mac." She looked confused at my request.

"First off they work for you too so you could have called them, but off that why would I have them follow Mac when we're looking for Marco?" I ran my hand down my face and explained the situation to her and why I had to leave the party; she shook her head and went on a five minute rant about snakes and loyalty.

Once we had that settled I called Jay to put him up on game and to keep a look out for anything suspicious. "Yo Jay, keep your eyes and ears open for anything out of the ordinary, don't even serve no one new, anything you feel ain't right, ain't right you feel me?" I didn't really have to give Jay much instruction, between the three of us shit just flowed.

"Say less, let me know when y'all get back, I never got to give little man my gift." I told him I would and we hung up.

"Mya, where are you at?" I went looking for her around our suite and I finally found her dry heaving over the toilet.

"I think I'm pregnant, I don't understand we had been so careful until the night of the party." She looked like she was really trying to figure out when I got her ass pregnant.

"Shit ma, you know we wild and random as fuck, plus let's be real the pull out method ain't exactly bullet proof. I'll call Esmeralda, and have her get you a text from the store." She nodded and I headed out the room.

I found Esmeralda in the kitchen, I told her to have it discreetly delivered to me or Mya and no one else. I didn't fuck with Cash at the moment, and I don't trust a nigga around my seed who won't even bother to see his own.

"Dre, come and walk with me." Ruiz spoke as he was headed out the door. I did a light jog to catch up with him, and I noticed a nigga was slightly out of shape.

"What can I do for you Senor Ruiz?" He chuckled slightly.

“I owe you an apology for multiple things, one of them being for blindsiding you and Mya with this marriage proposal.” I nodded as he continued talking. “When me and Cash first had this discussion he was the only option, because he told me he loved my niece and didn’t want anyone else, but now I can’t leave my operation in his hands. But, being a man of my word I can’t go back on it either, the other cartels have agreed that if you make our problem disappear then we leave everything to you, that is our only condition.

I rubbed my hands like birdman at what he was saying, but was curious at one thing. “Why the change of heart? You were willing to leave your empire to Cash, and now your just willing to give it to me, why? I needed to make sure I could trust him.

He laughed so hard his belly shook, “Dre, I am not leaving my organization to you, I am leaving it to Mya, but women are only allowed to run it if their spouse dies while in power, you understand. I also had a talk with Cash when he first woke up, he was more than happy to hear about Mya, even wanted me to call her, but he didn’t want Shawn. He said he didn’t want a kid and she knew that. I have no respect for a man who is all about the power and not his family.” I shook my head in disgust.

“Well that’s his fault, Mar’Shawn is a great kid, and will continue to be.” He nodded and we spent about an hour or so going over details for Arizona and the next shipment. I got to know Ruiz, and he was a cool ass dude. We smoked some good ass weed and I had some of the finest tequila, when I got back to our suite I was feeling more than good.

I hoped the shower and washed the day’s dirt off me before climbing in to bed with Mya, her ass didn’t play that shit at all. One time I got in the bed without showering and her ass through a whole fit, pulled the sheets off the bed the next day and washed them.

I grabbed my towel and wrapped it around my waist, and noticed three white sticks sitting on the cabinet, when I got closer they were pregnancy test. Looking at all three I saw they said positive. I was ecstatic as fuck, my baby was having my baby, no fuck that my baby was having my second baby.

"Mya, wake your ass up, why didn't you call me ma, wake up." She stirred and turned her ass over to go to sleep on the other side. I decided to let her sleep for now, but her ass was about to be irritated as fuck with me if the myths were true. I wanted my baby to look like me, so I was about to nag the fuck out of her.

Mya

The day came for us to have this meeting with my uncle and go back home . Boy was I happy, I missed my bad ass son so much. I missed him running away from me while I tried to bathe him, and I miss his little words.

"I'm ready to go home Dre, I miss our son." I pouted and he laughed.

"We about to go right now, just give your uncle this last hour and we out." I nodded and kissed his lips. I straddled him and kissed his neck, and whispered in his ear, "I want to join the mile high club when we head home." He laughed and smacked me on my ass and said, "let's go girl with your crazy ass."

I was about to speak but we were interrupted by a knock on the door. "Come in." I yelled out while getting off of Dre.

"Mya, can I talk to you for a minute, in private please?" Markell asked me. I rolled my eyes to respond until Dre gave me those play nice eyes.

"Yeah bro, you can talk to her mean ass, I'll be back babe." Dre said and kissed me. I rolled my eyes the minute he looked away, and without looking at me Dre said, "Stop rolling those damn eyes Mya, I can feel them." We both laughed because he just knew me.

"So what's up Markell, what do you want to talk about?" I asked him as I sat on the couch that was inside our room.

"Look, I want to apologize for how I came at you, and for this whole arrangement. I thought we would have been living life together as Bonnie and Clyde, not me falling into a coma, you having a baby and meeting a new nigga. A nigga that worked for me Mya, you literally fucking the help." He laughed at his own attempt of a joke.

"Are you finish Cash?" I called him Cash so he would know we have nothing personal discuss, anything personal between us was done.

"No Mya, I fucking love you, I love you and I don't want to live my life without you. I missed out on almost two years with you ma, let me try to get you back, you looked out for my mom's. She is in the best treatment facility known to man, you called and checked on a nigga every month. You recorded moments and sent me pictures for them to hang around my room. You and I are meant to be Mya, you my ride or die ma; it's us to the end."

I literally had tears running down my face, not because I missed him or wanted him back because not once did he mention my son, our son. He had a whole life planned that did not include him. I reached into the couch cushion and pulled out my gun, cocked it and put it under his chin before he even knew what was happening.

“Don’t you ever say you love me, because to love me is to love all of me, which includes my baby. I wasted tears for you, I have a body count that I’m sure exceeds yours because I made a whole fucking state bleed behind you. Dre tells my son about you every fucking night, and as I look at you now I see that you aren’t worth any of those things.”

“We will be seeing you again and soon, when I do it won’t be under the protection of the cartel, because I will be running the muthafucka, now get the fuck out of my room please, and close the door behind you.” I finished off with a smile, how dare that asshole even fix his mouth to say he loves anyone other than himself.

Markell

When I went in Mya’s room it wasn’t to profess my love to her, but I used that to my advantage. I overheard her and Dre talking about Marco and Mac working together, and as much as I hated my brother right now I needed his stupid ass to help me get Mya, my city and the country of Colombia under my control.

I called the last number I had for Mac, and waited on him to answer.

“Who’s this?” Mac sounded high as fuck, its damn shame when a nigga just sound lifted.

“It’s me, Markell.” I shook my head at my current situation.

“Well well well, what can I do for you? Last I heard you were laid up half way dead somewhere.” I could hear the envy dripping off his voice, as well as the hate.

“I need your help taking down Dre and Mya.”

“That’s all you had to say, I’ll send you my address you can meet me here in a few days.”

“Cool, I’ll see you then.” We ended the call and I felt as if I just made a deal with the devil all for greed but fuck it, I wanted my fucking empire back.

***

“Alright Dre, you already know but Mya and Markell don’t. Just so you know the other cartels want Marco gone, whoever takes him out has the blessing to marry Mya, and get to lead the family once I am no longer able.” Ruiz said, Mya and Dre smiled happily at each other as if they knew something I didn’t, but little did they know I was one step ahead of them.

“Cool, I’ll get on that soon as I can, but I will need to leave for the states ASAP.” I looked around the room and no one spoke up but Dre, “You are more than welcome to fly back with me and Mya, were about to head out in about forty five minutes though, so you would have to be packed by then.”

“Good looking Dre.” I said and we slapped hands.

Twenty minutes later I was all packed up, a nigga was feeling good. I was ready to get back control of these Cali streets, I had spent years building up my team, buying my traps and coming up with a system. I wasn’t about to let my ex bitch and her new nigga, especially a nigga that worked for me take that shit away.

“Alright y’all I’m ready to go.” I looked at Mya, who was wearing a netted dress with a highlighter yellow bikini underneath, but wore shorts so I couldn’t see her underwear. That shit reminded of me of the first time I brought out here.

"You can put your bags in that car, we're heading to my private air strip, so unfortunately theses two men are going to cover your head with this bag." Mya spoke, and when she snapped her fingers I was being held and a bag was indeed thrown over my face.

About five minutes later we were stopping and I was being guided on to the plane, when I finally had the bag taken from over my face, we'd already taken off. Mya and Dre were in front of me eating fucking strawberries and drinking champagne.

"Was all of that necessary Mya, I mean come on now we go way back." I was lightly hurt by her antics, who the fuck does she think she is to put a bag over my head. I'm the king of Cali!

Mya

"Well yes and no." He looked at me confused so I explained, "No, I didn't have to do it but I was watching a movie last night and I decided to try it, lighten up it was harmless fun, damn." Dre started to laugh and Markell, looked like he wanted to slap the fuck out of me.

"You trifling as fuck Mya, what the fuck happened to the nurse I met a couple years ago? You a crazy bitch now." He spoke with so much hatred.

"Look my guy, we got a long ass flight ahead of us, so you might want to cool it with the disrespect. Out of respect for this whole awkward ass situation I have stalled you out, but what you won't do is disrespect my wife with me sitting here." When he was done he had my panties soaked as fuck.

"Baby, can you come with me to the back room really quick?" I whispered in Dre's ear.

"Stop being petty Mya." He laughed so I pouted and sat there with an attitude.

“Damn, I remember that pout, trust me bruh it’s best to give her whatever it is she asking for because her ass get mean when she can’t get her way.” Markell said trying to be funny, not knowing that Dre was looking out for his sensitive ass.

“Damn, you right bruh we can’t have that, come on baby so I can give you what you want.” I jumped my ass out my seat and walked towards the room quickly, he sure didn’t have to tell my ass again.

I laid on the bed and took my netted top off, Dre stood over me and looked me in my eyes. “I love you Mya.” He kissed me hungrily and laid down next to me rubbing my flat ass stomach. “I love you too daddy.” I rubbed his hand as he rubbed my stomach, and we kind of just enjoyed the moment. “I want another boy, a junior maybe.” I said to Dre.

“Hell no we are not naming our son Drew, we’ll give him his own name, a name fit for a king.” I nodded and laughed because I couldn’t understand why Drew hated his name so much, that shit was regular as fuck.

“Okay, now go to sleep babe I’m tired as fuck.”

“I knew your little ass wasn’t about to do nothing but sleep anyway, you just wanted to be petty.”

“Whatever.”

***

We'd finally landed and we were all about to go our separate ways, my driver Aaron was already here to pick us up. I was beyond grateful because I missed my little man so much I couldn't wait to kiss on his little cheeks.

"Is the house in Palisades still ours or did you sale it?" I heard Markell say.

"No I kept it, I still have a few things there but I'll come and get them later on." I reached in my bag and pulled out the key. "The code to the gate is still your birthday, have a good night and don't even think about causing trouble Cash, these aren't the streets you ran, and you crew is dead and gone." I rolled my window up and drove off.

Thirty minutes later we pulled up to our home, and it was eerily quiet for about five minutes until I heard my baby's little footsteps, "Hey momma's boy." I scooped him up in my arms and just loved on him for a cool twenty seconds.

"Dada, Dada, Dada." I rolled my eyes because mommy couldn't even get a moment of love. "Let's go find Dada." I held his hand as we went to find Dre, when we finally found him he was in the garage putting away our suitcases.

"Dada, you back." I just smiled as Dre and Shawn interacted with one another.

"Dada always comes back." He said and gave him a big kiss. We spent the remainder of the day having a family day before all work came in to play.

Markell

I pulled up to my crib that I used to share with Mya, and the memories just came flooding back, the day we brought this house, to the day we headed to the warehouse together. I had a real life rida and I let her fucking get away.

I went through the refrigerator and it was stocked with a sticky note from Mya.

Markell,

I may not like you right now but I won't let you starve

Get yourself together and handle your business

Well to the best of your abilities because I always win

May the best one win!

-Mya

I laughed as I finished reading it because it was just so Mya, as I walked around the living room I saw photos of my son with both Mya and Dre, I felt like a fucking dead beat. I never wanted to be the nigga that had they son calling another nigga daddy, but that's exactly what I am.

I got upstairs to our bedroom and it smelled like Mya, as if she came herself and dusted this big muthafucka, I knew a part of her still loved me but I believe it left when she realized I didn't want kids and that I have been awake for five months.

In my room I saw stacks of movies that looked like hood nigga movies, I shook my head because I could see now how her and Dre, became her and Dre.

I couldn't stand being in this fucking house anymore, so I dipped out and called up Mac to let him know I was on my way.

"What's up bro?" Mac asked, as if we didn't have beef and he hadn't put me in a coma.

"What's up Mac, how you been?" I asked as I looked around his dumpy ass apartment. My brother looked to have taken a huge fall from grace.

"I been surviving, I hit a lick or two on Mya's stash houses, but I always come up short, her setup is good as fuck." He sounded pissed and impressed.

"Did she keep any of our old houses?" I could get back in the game all I needed was a few houses and soldiers.

"Nah, she burned all of them down, she also killed every nigga that worked for you, so getting a crew will be difficult." He ran his hand down his face in irritation.

"Okay, take me to a few of their spots, let me see the setup." He nodded and we hopped in his ride. I was ready to make my presence felt, Cali was about to realize you don't just get rid of the king.

Dre

"Alright Ms. Draught, by the look of your ultrasound you are approximately fourteen weeks pregnant." The doctor said as she printed our copies.

"So, when can we find out if I'm having another prince or my first princess?" I asked, I was happy as fuck and a nigga couldn't hide it, not that I wanted to anyway.

"Boy we got to wait at least four to six more weeks, right doc?" Mya's know it all ass asked.

"I'm afraid she's right, well go ahead and make your first appointment at the front desk or you can do it on your phone. I'll see you guys next time."

We were in the car heading over to the house when Mya got a call from Ricardo, one of her crazy ass Colombians we had watching Mac. We were meeting him at the warehouse, but just in case I hit Jay and told him to meet us there, so we could all be on one accord.

Pulling up to the warehouse Ricardo was already inside.

“Hello Dre, and Mya, I have been watching Mac, for a few days. I have a few other people watching him as well, so he doesn’t get used to one face, and so far the only person he has met up with is his brother Cash. They have also been talking on the phone and riding through your different traps.” My jaws clenched as I listened to him basically tell me that Cash, was planning to fuck me over big time.

“Where does Mac live?” Ricardo gave me the address and Mya, and I both decided to check it out for ourselves.

We got word out to our guys to keep their ears open, and I sent Jay to grab our new shipment. It was hard as fuck because I don’t know who wanted Mac and Cash dead more out of the three of us. Mac played a part in Jay getting tortured, and Cash wasn’t worried about his workers so he didn’t even know anything was up.

Mac killed Mya’s parents and tried to kill her, and Cash was basically saying fuck his own son, but wanted to kill Marco to marry her and take her family business. I just wanted to kill the niggas for all of the above, rid all of us of these fake ass want to be gangsters.

“Babe let’s use the new toys, what’s the point of buying them if we never going to use them? It’s a waste of money.” Mya preached, we had just recently went to a arms deal auction and Mya wanted to try out a few of our new guns, but I was waiting for a special moment.

“The day we kill Marco we can use the new toys, deal?”

"Deal." She turned on the radio and sung along to *Beyoncé and Jay-Z On The Run.*

I don't care if we on the run

Baby as long as I'm next to you

And if loving you is a crime

Tell me why do I bring out the best in you

I hear sirens while we make love

Loud as hell but they don't know

They're nowhere near us

I will hold your heart and your gun

I don't care if they come, no

I know it's crazy but

They can take me

Now that I found the places that you take, take me

Without you I got nothing to lose

She was singing that song as if she was Queen B herself, I rapped along with her as if I was Jay, these moments right here were what I was willing to kill a nigga over. I be damned if a nigga was rapping and acting silly with the woman I was meant to spend the rest of my life with.

"Why are you staring at me like that?" I asked Mya.

"Because there is no one else in this world I would rather go kill a nigga with." She said and blew me a kiss as if shit was normal.

“Right back at cha ma.” I looked at her and she was happy as fuck, some days I would forget that I was in love with a Queen Pin, hell her ass was thugged out as fuck, but still laid back.

“Baby, I want to take Shawn to Chucke E Cheese when we get all of this settled. I just want him to have as much fun as possible before shit gets hectic, which it will soon. If we kill Marco we become Ruiz, we will be running a major cartel and that’s not easy.” I listened to her vent and I could see her mind running a mile a minute, so I grabbed her hand and kissed the back of it basically telling her to relax.

***

We finally pulled up to Mac’s block and was looking out the window, the tints on my truck was dark as fuck, so I didn’t have to worry about anyone seeing me or Mya big headed ass.

We had been sitting outside of Mac’s house for about three hours and nothing so far, not one car nor a light had turned on or gone off.

“Babe, we are going to have to separate, you watch Mac’s house and I’ll go watch Markell’s place, if they’re meeting up as often as Ricardo was saying I’m sure it won’t be in this dump, especially with Markell having a whole mansion.” I listened to what she said, but I couldn’t send my pregnant fiancé into the lion’s den, hell nah.

“I’ll go and you stay here and watch Mac’s place.” I tried to reason with her.

“Baby no, I know every nook and cranny in that house, plus I know the codes and where the cameras are.”

“I know where the guns are.”

"So do I." We were going back and forth so we called Ricardo to sit on Mac's house, and called Jay to ride with us to the house in Palisades. Jay pulled up at the same time as us and was out the car with his gun locked and loaded ready to go, we each had two guns in our hands and extra clips.

"Okay, look Marco is specially trained for shit like this, he's taught me a few things since I've been back and forth to Colombia, so I'll take him if he's here and y'all handle Markell and Mac, sounds like a plan?" Mya asked, well said because it sounded more like an order than a request.

"Don't do no extra shit, think of Shawn and our other young prince or princess you hear me Mya?" She nodded and I grabbed her face and kissed her.

We went around the back of the house and took the back entrance that leads in to the basement, Mya put the code in and we went through the gate. When we got inside we heard muffled voices coming from upstairs, since we were unsure which part of the house they were in we all had to split up.

"I love you Mya, you and my son, don't try to do no extra shit." She nodded I turned toward Jay and dapped him up, that nigga had become like a brother to me. "Stay safe bro, fuck these niggas up and get the fuck out, we don't offer no medical benefits." Jay chuckled and Mya popped both of our asses in the back of the head.

"Damn, can't y'all niggas anywhere, let's go damn." Mya said and walked her ass away from us, we shook our heads and followed behind her.

Mya

I left Dre and Jay's ass because just like niggas they could never take shit seriously, I went down the hall that led to the foyer, while Dre went upstairs toward the room, and Jay went toward the living and dining rooms.

As I got to the office I heard voices that sounded like Mac and Markell, I took a deep breath and kicked the door in, I shot Mac in his stomach and he went down slowly. Markell hid behind the desk and was yelling, "So that's what we come to Mya, you trying to kill a nigga? You don't love me no more ma?" You going to explain to our son that you killed me when he asks about his real father?" I tried to block out what he was saying, but he was pulling on my heart strings.

"You don't even care about my son Markell, you haven't even seen him, heard his little voice, I'll let you go if you tell me where Marco is." I knew that was a lie but fuck it, it was worth a shot.

"He's on his way now ma, I used these niggas to get to Marco, I would have never tried to kill your ass like you doing me." He sounded so hurt. He stood up from behind the desk and pointed my gun toward him.

"Don't come near me Markell, I'm not fucking with you." I tried not to cry, at one point he was my world and now he's just nothing.

"Shoot me Mya, if you don't love me shoot me." He said as he walked toward me. The tears started to fall and my vision became blurry, my hands started to shake.

"Don't come any closer Markell, I'm fucking serious, I don't want to but I will shoot your ass." I said it so loudly I'm sure Dre heard me.

Markell didn't listen and kept walking towards me, so I pulled the trigger hitting him in the shoulder. "Fuck! Mya you fucking shot me ma." The pain in his eyes tugged at my heart and I regretted it. I didn't want to kill Markell, but I couldn't trust his ass.

"I told you not to come near me and you wouldn't listen, you never fucking listen." He looked at me with so much hatred in his eyes.

"You a dead bitch Mya, you might as well kill me now." I raised my gun to shoot him again and the next thing I know I was shot from behind. I looked down and blood was coming from my stomach.

"My baby." I cried out as I held my bleeding stomach, I couldn't remember anything after that because everything went black.

Dre

I was upstairs trying to see if anyone was up hear when I heard Mya scream, "My baby." I hurried down the stairs and saw Jay hurrying toward the same direction, once I hit the bottom step bullets started flying from everywhere. I tried to take cover but the downstairs was to open, I could hear voices but couldn't make out what they were saying.

I saw them carrying a figure out of the office and I noticed it was Mya, with blood coming from her stomach. "Jay they got Mya, we can't let these niggas get up out of here." I yelled out, he nodded and we start dropping niggas left and right.

"Mya." I yelled out to her, but wasn't getting an answer. We finally dropped all the niggas that were in the foyer, and headed out the door where they took Mya. When we made it outside there wasn't anyone out there, just headlights at the end of the block. "Fuck!" I yelled out.

“Let’s go man, let’s try to catch them niggas before they get to far.” Jay said, we hopped in the car and drove for miles but couldn’t catch them, they’d vanished and had my wife. Thinking of the blood that was coming from her stomach, I think lost my wife and my baby.

“Fuck! Jay man. Fuck!” I repeatedly banged my fist in to the dashboard of Jay’s car, my life was gone. We had a son to raise, another on the way, an empire to build and vacations to take.

Two Weeks Later…

I had torn the streets of Los Angeles up looking for Mya, or any of those niggas and couldn’t find shit. It was as if they all just vanished, my son constantly asked for his mother and I had nothing to tell him. My mom and dad he begun to keep him more because I wasn’t all the way together to care for another human being.

I looked down at my phone and it was Ruiz calling, he had been calling me for days and I just couldn’t speak, but I decided to say fuck it and finally answer the phone.

“Hello Senor Ruiz.” I spoke while rubbing my hand down my face.

“Ah so he answers today, I have been trying to reach you with information and you have been avoiding me.” I could hear the disappointment in his voice and I felt like shit.

“I do apologize Ruiz, what information you got for me?” I asked him hoping it had something to do with Mya.

“Our private doctor we have in California was killed two weeks ago along with his team, his wife says they had him assist a woman who came in with a shot to the stomach.” My ears perked up at the thought of Mya being alive and maybe even my child.

“When did you come by this information?” I felt like shit for avoiding him knowing he had information on my wife.

“I’ve had this information for a few days Dre, but it doesn’t matter, find my niece and bring my little man to come see me, I will continue to supply you and you must continue to raise him how you have been.” I nodded as if he could see me before agreeing and ending our call, I would always hold out hope for Mya, and continue to look for her but I had to pull myself together for my son.

Markell

I stared at her as she slept and rested so peacefully, she should have known I wouldn’t let her run off and marry the fucking help. When Marco, shot Mya, in the stomach she lost consciousness from hitting her head on the way down. When we took Mya, we had no idea she was pregnant, but what was more interesting was that she was apparently pregnant with twins and only one of them survived.

The irony that Dre, is raising my son and I would be raising his is a crazy beautiful thing, I would have the family he so desperately wanted.

The best part about all of this was Mya, had been experiencing memory loss from her hit to the head, the doctors didn’t know whether it would be permanent or temporary, but as long as I kept her away from anything that would jog her memory she would be fine.

We were currently in Montego Bay, Jamaica while Mya was recovering, Marco had contacts out here with a few people who are willing to pay good money for the death of dear ole Ruiz

Escobar. They wanted his fields, and in order for that to happen they needed him gone. The fact that he had no sons, they would rather take him out now then have to kill his daughters at a later date.

As I was lost in my thoughts Mya, began to stir. “Where am I?” She asked in a groggy voice.

“Hey baby, we’re on vacation in Jamaica.” I said, she tried to sit up and I laid her back down because she still couldn’t move too much yet.

“You have to take it easy ma, our baby needs for you to relax.” The look on her face was comical.

“Ha ha very funny Markell, but I am not pregnant.” She rolled her eyes at me and I’d be lying if I said I didn’t miss that feisty ass attitude.

“You are though ma.” I explained everything to her about losing one of the twins, but left out the part about a shooting because I didn’t want to cause her to get a memory back. She began to cry and I held her as she cried in to my shoulder.

About an hour later she finished crying, and we were watching movies on BET when Boyz in the hood came on and she got really hyped, “Babe this is your movie.” I looked her and was lost as fuck.

“Girl I hate this fucking movie.” She looked at me confused and that’s when it hit me this must be that nigga Dre’s movie. I rubbed my hand down my face because this was going to be harder than I thought.

Mya

Three years later

I was cruising down the highway singing along with the radio while glancing in the mirror at my handsome son Cairo, I have no idea why I decided to name him that but it just stuck to me. My baby was a true momma's boy, and if I left the house he was right there with me.

"Momma, I wanna go swim." Cairo, said from the backseat. My husband Markell, and I had moved to San Diego a few months ago, and every time he saw the water his little ass wanted to go swim in it.

"Okay baby, let's go to the store first."

"Cookies! Cookies! Cookies!." He yelled and clapped his hands. I swear they invented the cookie monster just because of his little bad ass.

When we got to the store I got him out and began grocery shopping when someone crashed in to my basket.

"My bad ma, I apologize." A man said I looked in to his eyes and I swore he looked so familiar.

"Umm that's okay I need to pay closer attention to where I'm going." I said as tried to walk away.

"So you really just going to walk away from a nigga like you don't know me?" The stranger said.

"I'm sorry I don't know you." I said just as my son made his presence known.

"Mommy cookies."

"Wow he looks just like Dre." The man said

I grabbed my son and held him, "Look, I don't know who you are but leave me the hell alone." I tried to walk off and he grabbed me.

"The name is King." He said as he walked off. I grabbed a few things from the store and ran my ass up out of there. I was racking my brain trying to remember a King but I just couldn't, since Jamaica there were still parts of my memories I couldn't access.

I finally arrived home and got everything ready for dinner, changed Cairo, in to his swim clothes and went to forget about the weird ass trip to the store.

Dre

"I want this one daddy." Shawn bad ass said as we went in the third toy store of the day.

"Grab it and let's go." I swear that boy was four going on fourteen with his bad ass. As I got to the checkout line my phone ringing brought me out of my thoughts.

"What's up King, it's been a minute nigga you better be lucky the number still the same." He laughed at me.

"Drop whatever the fuck you doing my boy, and get to Diego now." He said in a urgent tone.

"Why what's going on?" I needed to know anything before leaving my son, I just got back from a trip to Colombia so I didn't want to leave him again.

"I just saw Mya and your son nigga, she didn't even remember me, I just followed her to her house, they living with that mark ass nigga Cash." It was as if time stopped for a minute because I know this nigga didn't just say Mya, had my son and was living with Cash, bitch ass.

"I'm on the way."

To be continued….

CPSIA information can be obtained
at www.ICGtesting.com
Printed in the USA
LVHW111336190520
656059LV00001B/286

9 781795 670654